Toby Tuttles
And The
Lost Temple

David Chantala

authorHOUSE®

AuthorHouse™
1663 Liberty Drive
Bloomington, IN 47403
www.authorhouse.com
Phone: 1 (800) 839-8640

Published by AuthorHouse 05/12/2016

ISBN: 978-1-5246-0666-4 (sc)
ISBN: 978-1-5246-0664-0 (hc)
ISBN: 978-1-5246-0665-7 (e)

Library of Congress Control Number: 2016907741

Print information available on the last page.

Any people depicted in stock imagery provided by Thinkstock are models, and such images are being used for illustrative purposes only. Certain stock imagery © Thinkstock.

This book is printed on acid-free paper.

Contents

Chapter 1

The Road Trip

Toby shoved the last bite of toast, dripping with red jelly into his mouth then leaned back in his chair. Breakfast had been a makeshift meal consisting of whatever you wanted to fix. He had a large bowl of sugar coated corn flakes, toast with lots of jelly and a glass of milk. His dad, mom and sister Heather were all busy scurrying around the house getting ready for a road trip to New Orleans. His sister's "Cheer" team was in a final competition there and his folks had volunteered to take Heather and two of her friends to the meet.

Toby had requested to stay home and tend to the house and yard while they were gone. There was no way he wanted to be the only guy there among a bunch os screaming girls.

He heard his mom call to his sister upstairs, "Hurry up honey, we need to be getting on the road soon."

"I'll be right down mom."

He heard the patter of several feet coming down the stairs. Toby stood up and walked into the living room which was a big mistake. Heather was carrying a couple of bags with her costume and shoes in them.

She looked at Toby and smiled, "You're just in time, would you be a dear and run up to my room and grab my suitcase. It's quite heavy and you're much stronger than I am."

Toby thought for a moment, "Oh sure, I'll bet you probably crammed a lot of junk in it you don't need."

Just then his dad stuck his head in the door, "Go help your sister with her luggage, we need to get rolling."

"Yes sir" Toby muttered and started up the stairs. He could hear his sister laughing.

"He is so gullible, almost always has to do everything I ask. If he hesitates mom or dad will usually make him do it." The three girls all giggled and went out the door.

Toby got to Heather's room and grabbed the purple suitcase that was waiting for him on her neatly made bed. It felt very heavy. Toby said quietly out loud, "What does she have in here, bricks." He unzipped the overstuffed parcel to have a look at what she was taking. It was stuffed with clothes, and right on the very top of everything was a new pair of blue jeans. Toby grinned, he carefully lifted the new jeans out and placed them in Heather's bottom dresser drawer. Then he quietly went to his parents room and selected a pair of his dad's old work jeans that he wore when working around the yard. He neatly folded them and laid them on top of the pile of clothes, then somehow managed to get the poor, overstuffed suitcase zipped closed. He grabbed the handle and pulled it off the bed, and just in time.

He heard heather holler, "Are you coming down or do I need to send dad up to help you?"

"I'm on my way right now, this thing is really heavy you know."

He drug the suitcase to the stairs and kind of let it slide down while he guided it, then carried it out the front door to the new ATV. His mom, dad, two girls and heather were all waiting by the rear of the vehicle, discussing the upcoming venture. His dad carefully placed the bag in the rear of the vehicle and closed the hatch.

"O K" "Everyone on board so we can get going." He looked at Toby, "I'm trusting you to take care of things while we're gone, you're getting to be a fine young man and I know I can depend on you."

His mom gave him a big hug, "If you have any problems or need anything you can call Allen's mom. She knows we're going to be gone for nine days."

"I'll be fine mom." He looked at Heather, "Good luck in the competition." She smiled and said thanks. Toby watched as the ATV vanished down the road, a little happy and a little sad. He liked the idea of being on his own for a few days but knew he was going to miss his mom, dad, and maybe even Heather.

He walked into the house, laid on the couch and thought about his first venture to Duppland, the new friends he made there and the treasure he had brought back and buried in the garden. His mom and dad were so excited after they dug it up and were told that they could keep it because it was unclaimed. Even though it made them quite wealthy they never flaunted it. They did buy a new ATV since their car was getting old and not reliable any more. His mom also got new furniture for the living room and kitchen which made her very happy. Toby was pleased that he was able to make these things possible even though he couldn't tell anyone that he brought the treasure back from Duppland and buried it in the garden for his folks to find. He had kept his promise to Lady Zelda that it would be their secret. He closed his eyes and happily dozed off.

"Toby!", "Toby!", "Help me!", "Help me!"

Toby jumped up and looked around. He was sure he had heard his friend Rain calling him. There was no one in the living room so he slowly walked into the kitchen. There was no one there either. He shook his head, walked over to the refrigerator and got a can of cold soda, snapped the tab and took a big swallow. "Guess I was just dreaming" he said out loud. He looked out the back door. The sun was shining bright and there were only a few white fluffy clouds in the sky that reminded him of giant balls of cotton floating around. He could see the sun reflecting off the pond in the park and decided to walk down to it. Maybe he would run into Allen or some of his other friends there.

He locked the front door then the back and placed the key in his own special hiding place. He promised his parents to never leave the house unlocked when no one was there. He started down the pathway to the park and the pond where he liked to hang out and sometimes skip rocks on its smooth surface. He got to the edge of the pond and watched as some gold colored fish swam lazily about. On the other side of the pond there was a man playing with a black dog. He would toss a stick and the dog would run and grab it then bring it back so it's owner could throw it again. There was no one else in the park.

Toby looked at the reflections on the water. He could see himself and the tree behind him, then he froze for a moment. Standing next to him in the reflection was a tall, nice looking lady with dark hair and wearing a blue and purple dress. He slowly turned around.

"Hello Toby, do you remember me?"

"Yeah, sure, you're Lady Laura. You kind of took me by surprise."

She smiled. "I'm glad you still remember me, its been quite some time since we last spoke. I know you have been to Duppland several times since then to visit Boggs and Rain but I never had a chance to see or talk to you. Your stays were always short and I was always busy with other matters while you were there. Anyway the reason I am here is because Lady Zelda says it is imperative that she sees you as soon as possible. It's a matter of great importance, Are you able to come?"

"Yeah, sure, my parents will be gone for eight or nine days and I can do whatever I choose while they're away". He tried to sound older and in charge of himself to impress Lady Laura.

"Good" she said very seriously, "come on, we need to hurry." He followed her to the large oak tree and the awaiting portal that connected their two worlds.

Chapter 2

The Impossible Mission

Toby followed Lady Laura through a heavy wooden door marked private. It opened into a large drab room with no furniture except for a ugly wooden desk. Behind it was a very uncomfortable looking chair with a high straight back, and there was a long wooden bench the full length of the desk in front of it.

Lady Laura looked at Toby, "Please do not seat yourself, I shall inform Lady Zelda that you are waiting."

"Yes ma'am" Toby said softly.

Laura quietly disappeared from the room, softly closing the door behind her. Toby looked around, all four walls were painted the same dull bluish color with dark grey trim. The floor was a natural colored, heavily grained wood with no carpeting or area rugs. There were no wall hangings except for one large mirror carefully placed so that whoever was sitting behind the desk would have a full view of the entry door in its image.

After a couple of minutes Lady Zelda appeared, walked over to Toby, smiled and shook his hand.

"I am very glad you were able to come on such short notice, please sit down," she pointed to the uninviting bench at the front of her desk.

"Thank you" Toby said softly and positioned himself at the center of it and sat. There was a moment or two of silence while Zelda shuffled some papers in front of her then slid them aside and looked Toby straight in the eye.

"We, Rain and myself need your help. Rain is in a very bad way which could have lasting effects on every young lady here in Duppland."

Toby looked puzzled, "What do you mean?"

Zelda looked down at her desk, then back up at Toby, then she stood up. "She has been taken prisoner by Dr. Zodd and is being held captive in his private temple. She is to be sacrificed to a hideous living stone creature on the night of the first full moon in June."

Toby looked up at Zelda, "That's this month in only in three or four days." He paused for a second, "It's weird, only this morning I dreamed that she was calling me to help her. It was so real that it woke me up."

Zelda shook her head, "That was no dream, she was calling to you telepathically. She strongly believes that you are the only person she knows who cares enough, is brave enough, and cunning enough to save her from the evil clutches of Dr. Zodd."

Toby shook his head, "I wouldn't even know where to start. Why is she to be sacrificed anyway, and how could she communicate with me telepathically or any other way since we both live worlds apart?"

Zelda smiled a little, "Telepathic communication has been used for centuries. Here in Duppland it enables someone to communicate with another without the use of manual or electronic devices. You heard Rains cries for help while sleeping, but you probably would have heard them even if you were awake and not involved in some distractive activity. The reason for the sacrifice is a long story, It all began when Dr. Zodd and the other twelve witches crossed over to this land some four hundred years ago. One of the witches named Abbey was attracted to him and would do anything to please him. She had left two daughters behind which she missed very much so Dr Zodd told her she needed to go back through the portal and bring them to this new land. Abbey obeyed and returned with her two daughters, the oldest named Jewel and the younger named Crystal. Dr Zodd found Crystal to be extremely attractive with dark hair and blazing green eyes. Even though he was quite older than she he forced his affections on her and declared to all the nations of the northlands that Crystal was to be hailed as the Emerald Princess because of her emerald green eyes, and that she would become the Emerald Queen and his new bride on the day of the first full moon in June."

"This forceful union made the Emerald Princess, (Crystal) very unhappy. She had no feelings for the evil Dr. and prayed that the marriage would never take place. Dr. Zodd decided that he would give her a gift that no one else could give her. He knew that she had studied Greek Mythology and was fascinated by a hideous creature called a Minotaur, a monster with the body of a bull and the head and shoulders of a gruesome man with long fangs and sharp horns." "The legend says that it would kill and eat whatever was sacrificed to it, leaving only the bones of its victims behind. It supposedly lived in a dark maze inside a cave and could see its prey in the dark. Once a victim entered the maze there was no way out except past the Minotaur."

"Dr. Zodd believed that if he created a living stone replica of this creature that lived in a dark maze accessible only from inside his private temple and presented it to his beloved bride on the eve of their wedding that she would feel some of the love and emotion for him that he had for her. When she heard of the unearthly gift the Dr. had created for her, she secretly entered into the maze on the eve of their wedding day, and rather than being forced to marry Dr. Zodd she chose death. She flung herself into the path of the charging Minotaur and was devoured by the very creature that the Dr. had created to help win her love."

"Dr. Zodd was enraged and heart broken at the same time. He hid the entrance to the temple so that no one could find it unless the location was given to them. He also placed one of his faithful giants to guard the exit from the maze so that no one could get out, even if they managed to get by the stone monster. Since that time, every year on the eve of his fabled wedding day, a sacrifice has been offered to the evil monster. Until now it has always been a pig or a goat. This year Dr. Zodd proclaimed that the sacrifice would be a young female of pure quality, and the same for every year hereafter. So you can see how important it is that you rescue Rain and stop these sacrifices from happening in the future." "Rain must be rescued!"

"I know it's a big responsibility to give to a lad who is only fifteen years old, but you've seemed mature for your age, and there is no one here in Duppersville who is brave enough or cunning enough to even begin such a challenge. Howsever myself and a couple of the quorum can give you a little edge over some of the pearls you're likely to run into."

Toby looked at Zelda, "A little edge, what would that be?"

"Follow me."

Chapter 3

Secrets Revealed

Toby followed Zelda out into the courtyard. There Boggs, Master Diggers, Lady Dana and Lady Laura were waiting. Boggs was holding a long wooden staff made of a very dark looking wood. Lady Zelda, her two aides, Boggs, and Master Diggers all placed their hands on the staff, looked directly at it and spoke.

"We command you to protect your bearer at all times." One by one they released the staff and stepped back. Boggs walked over to Toby and handed him the staff.

"Here, you need to keep this next to you at all times. It is made from Ironwood, it is very strong, not heavy at all and it's very rare. There are only two such trees of this type in all of Duppland so you must take care not to lose it."

Toby looked at the staff and nodded.

Master Diggers walked over to Toby, "Here, I want you to have this". It was a brown, leather pouch with a long leather strap. He slipped the strap over Toby's head and the pouch hung neatly at his side.

Toby looked a little puzzled, "What's in it?"

Diggers smiled, "It's phosphorus dust, you know, that stuff that glows in the dark. It's actually quite handy, on dark nights you can drop a pinch or so of the stuff and it shows where you have been. If you toss a handful of it into the air, it kind of explodes making a very bright blueish flash that slowly fades away after it settles back to the ground. It might come in handy if you need to travel when its very dark."

Toby nodded then stepped back a couple of steps and looked at the small group who were all looking back at him. "Now that I am armed with a stick and a bag of dust will someone tell me where I am supposed to go?"

Zelda looked serious and shook her head, "No one really knows. All that we are sure of is that Rain is being held captive in Dr. Zodd's temple. Its referred to as the lost temple because no one knows exactly where it is. Rumors have it that the old hermit of hidden gulch may know the way. You will need to find him and perhaps, if he's in a good mood, he will tell you how to get there."

Toby shrugged and shook his head, "Just how do I get to hidden gulch?"

Zelda shook her head, "No one is really sure, it is believed that if you take the forbidden trail at the end of the street by the park, you know, the one that you and Rain took into the forest of Haggardly when the two of you were following the shadow people a couple of years ago. Well just before you get to the clearing where the firepit and the forever burning embers are glowing you need to turn left on a path that leads to the north and out of the forest. The path is hard to see because it is seldom used and is overgrown with shrubs, weeds, fallen branches and other litter. Once you are out of the forest you will come to the Badlands of Axmar. There you will need to wait till just after the sun goes down and it is almost dark. If you look to the north you can sometimes see the glow of the old hermits campfire on the wall of hidden gulch off in the distance. Once you spot it you will need to go swiftly towards it, but you will need to be careful not to trip over or fall into one of the many traps that have been sat there by the north people. If you don't reach hidden gulch before the fire goes out it will be almost impossible to find it again. Once you get there you will need to give the hermit some sort of gift so that he will give you the directions you need to find the lost temple. The community cooks have prepared a bag of cookies to give him, after all, everyone loves cookies. They have also prepared a bag of food for you to take, some biscuits, jerky and some dried fruit."

"Also", Zelda continued, "I have commissioned two of the Elite Guardsmen to accompany you on your trek. They should be able to help fend off any assailants you encounter along the way." She raised her hand and snapped her fingers, two very large, over weight men appeared. They were wearing dark pants tucked into high leather boots, green shirts with long puffy sleeves, funny looking beret styled hats and long sabers hanging from their waste. They looked to be dressed more for a parade than a journey into the unknown. Zelda pointed to each, "This one is Olaf and that one is Garr." They each nodded to Toby.

Toby nodded back and thought "Boy, I sure hope we don't do anything to get their outfits dirty, their wives would probably have a fit. They probably think I don't look like much of a commander, dressed in a green long sleeved polo shirt with a red T-shirt over it, blue jeans, tennis shoes and armed with a stick and a bag of dirt. And just think, I'm leading these two "Super Warriors" into the unknown, wow."

Boggs looked up at the sun, "Its still early afternoon, If you start now you can probably make it to the wasteland outside the forest of Haggardly by sundown. I wish I was going with you to help save my granddaughter but I am old, slow and tire easily. I'm sure I would be more of a burden than a help to you. I'm sure you will do everything possible to save her, and she assures me that you are the best choice for the task." "Thank you."

Toby thought, "She says?" oh yeah, telepathic stuff.",

Zelda looked at Toby, "Do you understand what it is that you need to do now. If you think it's too dangerous and don't want to try it we will understand, it's quite an undertaking."

Toby nodded, "It is a challenge all right and it sounds pretty exciting to me, I'm willing to take a shot at it." He wouldn't admit to Zelda that he was scared to death, "So", he continued, "All I need to do is get through the forest of haggardly before dark, then find hidden gulch in the dark, get directions to the lost temple of Dr. Zodd from an old hermit, find Rain in a dark maze inside the temple, somehow get past the evil minotaur lurking somewhere in that maze, and if we finally find a way out I will need to best the giant guard who is not to let anyone pass. This might be a little more than just a walk in the park." They both smiled, Zelda knew he was referring to his first undertaking in Dupeland's haunted park two years earlier.

Chapter 4

Away We Go

Toby adjusted the pouch of phosphorus dust so that it sat more comfortable at his side, slid the strap holding the bag of food over his other shoulder, took the walking stick in his right hand, looked back at the two elite guards and uttered softly, "well, I guess we need to get started." He walked slowly down the street that would take him past the park entrance and to the forbidden pathway that led into the dense forest oh haggardly. He could hear the two elite guards plodding along a few feet behind him like a couple of old horses.

He turned onto the trail leading into the woods, paused for a moment, looked at the sign saying that it was closed, then ducked his head and started down the pathway. He carefully picked his way, being careful not to trip over any branches or shrubs laying across the trail. He used his walking stick to help pick his way, pushing aside some of the undergrowth that blocked the three venturers forward progress. That's when Toby started to realize that the walking stick was guiding him more than he was guiding it. He thought back about how Zelda and the others had all placed their hands on it and told it to protect him at all times. Now it was doing just that. It was as if it had some magical power that was controlling it. Toby had thought their little show was just for his benefit, but now he was wondering if there wasn't more to it, like maybe a little witchcraft and magic?

Ahead on the trail Toby could see the clearing where the never ending embers continued to slowly burn and glow in the firepit. He started looking to the left side of the trail for the path that would lead them out of the forest and to the edge of the badlands of Axmar. Just before they got to the clearing and the fire pit he spotted a narrow pathway, overgrown with all kinds of shrubs and bushes. He turned onto the trail and let his walking stick guide them through the tangled mess of vegetation. After what seemed like hours of dodging tree branches while picking his way through the entanglement of undergrowth and hearing the two overweight guards cursing at the obstacle course they were trying to maneuver, he was able to make out the barren waste land of Axmar ahead. The three of them walked out onto the clearing just as the sun was starting to slip below the horizon.

Toby looked back at the two guards, "It won't be long now."

"Yeah! Yeah!" came their sarcastic reply

Toby stood on his tiptoes to see as far across the waste lands as he could, hoping to get a glimpse of the hermits fire glowing on one of the walls of the many gulches ahead. It was getting quite dark when he spotted the faint, yellowish glow off in the distance.

Toby called back to the guards, "I think I've spotted it, it's right below that bright star ahead. If we walk towards it, it should lead us to the old hermits camp."

The two guards slowly got to their feet while mumbling about the dangers of wandering around the wastelands in the dark. Toby thought, "I sure hope these two are better in combat than they are at just walking around and doing nothing." Toby looked at the glow on the rim of the ravine ahead and the bright star above it. He was satisfied this was the right direction and headed towards it. He used his walking stick, probing their way in the darkness so that the three venturers would not trip or fall into some unknown hazzard hidden by the black veil of night that had surrounded them.

Every so often he would catch the sight of two glowing yellowish eyes off to his right that seemed to be stalking them. This made Toby very uneasy but he thought it would be best if he didn't mention it to the two cumbersome oafs struggling to keep up behind him. After what seemed like hours of slowly picking their way through the darkness the trio came to the edge of a deep ravine. Toby could still see the faint glow of a campfire on the wall of a gully just on the other side. Off to his right he could see the pale glow of the moon starting to come up over the horizon. He knew it would be almost a full moon and its bright glow would probably make the dim, flickering glow on the wall of the gully ahead vanish. He needed to figure out a way to get across the deep ravine before this happened.

He started walking along the edge hoping to find a place where they could climb down and get across the deep barrier. Finally he spotted a large tree that had fallen across it.

"Hey, come on" he called. "I found a way to cross."

The two guards walked over to the tree and looked at it. "Not me" said one, "Me neither" said the other. "You go ahead and cross on that and we'll find another way across then catch up with you on the other side."

Toby nodded and slowly started walking across the tree, using his walking stick for balance the way circus performers do when walking a tight rope. About half way across he could feel the tree start to sag a little because of his weight. He started to walk a little faster, got to the other side then jumped off. The two guards were right he thought, that tree wouldn't hold either one of then without breaking. Somehow he knew he would not see the two would-be warriors again.

He looked towards the dim glow of light that was still visible on the on the upper rim of the gully just ahead. He took a couple of steps then froze in his tracks. There were two pair of yellowish looking eyes glaring at him just a few feet in front of him. He could also hear growling coming from behind him. He could make out the forms of two large, vicious looking creatures crouched, down, their white fangs glowing in the moonlight and ready to leap at their prey. Toby was surrounded. With one of the beast snarling just behind him and the two in front ready to pounce on their prey gave hin no way to move in any direction. He held his walking stick out in front of him to try to fend off the predators attack that was sure to come. He stood there, his teeth chattering and his knees shaking, he felt weak and helpless as he waited. Then suddenly both savage looking creatures sprang into the air at the same time right at Toby, their eyes blazing and their mouths opened wide.

Suddenly the right side of his walking stick whipped around with lightning speed and caught the first predator squarely along the side of the head sending it tumbling to the ground. Then it whipped around to the left with so much force it almost pulled out of Toby's hands, smashing the second predator along its entire right side sending it flying several feet through the air and over the edge of the gully. Toby turned around just in time to see the third predator scurrying away as quick as it could. He looked at his staff and said out loud, "Wow!, what kind of magic did they give you." He shook his head and started towards the dim glow of the hermits campfire, half puzzled and half excited over his encounter with real danger.

Chapter 5

Hermits and Loners

Toby walked up to the still smouldering camp fire and looked around. There was no one in sight, but he could smell the faint odor of some kind of roasted meat.

"Hello the camp" he called softly, "Is anyone around?"

"Who are you and why are you here" a voice whispered loudly.

Toby peered into the darkness in the direction the voice came from. "My name is Toby, Toby Tuttles and I need to ask for some directions." The form of an old man slowly appeared from out of the darkness and moved near the campfire. He was wearing a ragged looking shirt, trousers cut off at the knees and no shoes. He had long grey hair and a short greyish beard.

"And what makes you think I might give you directions just like that. I don't know you and have never even heard of you," His reply was sharp and sarcastic.

Toby held out the parcel of cookies, "I have brought a small gift in exchange for some directions, these are some fresh baked cookies just made today. I'm sure you will like them."

The old man reached out and grabbed the box, "Well young lad, I've never eaten a cookie I didn't like. What is it you need to know?"

Toby swallowed hard, "I need to know how to find the Lost Temple of Dr. Zodd."

"What is it that makes you think I might know where it is, or that I would tell you even if I did.? It's a very bad place and you'd best stay away from it."

Toby looked down, "well a very good friend of mine is being held there and is to be sacrificed to some sort of evil monster in two or three days. I need to rescue her but no one in Duppland knows the whereabouts of the temple. I was told by the elders of the community that the hermit of hidden gulch was probably the only person around who might have any idea how to get there."

The old man looked straight at Toby, "First of all I'm not a hermit, I'm a loner. Hermits don't like other people, Loners, like myself, just don't want to be bothered by other people. There's a big difference, yeah, a big difference. Anyway, I can't tell you how to get there, but if it's that important to you I might be able to tell you how to find it."

Toby nodded wondering what the difference was, "Anything would be a big help, I don't have much time before she is to be sacrificed." The old loner could feel the fear in Toby's voice. He picked up a slim stick and smoothed out the dirt in front of him, then he drew a zig-zagged line in it.

"We are here", he made a small dot with his stick, "If you go straight east from here you will come to the ice desert of Voo. You must be very careful while crossing it. There are pits of quick sand and ice covered waste water. Both are impossible to get out of if you get caught in one. The way across is not very far but you must go slow. Always remember, when the way is slow, the earth will be patient. Once you cross the ice desert you will come to a forest with no name, here you will need to go north again. There is a pathway that will lead you straight through it, but you must not dally. This is a evil, wicked forest filled with many dangers. There are huge flowers with tentacle like leaves that will grab you and pull you into it's giant blossoms. Then they will close in around you, crushing you and eventually devouring you."

"Once you get through the forest you will be able to see the twin towers of Essor. When you reach them you will need to wait till sunset. Once the sun is directly behind them, their shadows will show on the stone cliffs of Morax. You will need to pay close attention to the location of these two shadows because it is believed that the entrance to the lost temple is somewhere in the cliffs between the two shadows."

Toby looked up at the loner, "Wow, it doesn't sound very easy does it. I had two helpers who came with me but I think they turned around on the other side of that deep ravine back there. I don't think they would have been much help anyway, they had a hard time keeping up when I was going slow.

"The old loner held up his hand, "There is an old saying, "Sometimes three is too many if one is enough." Always remember that. Also remember that after you rescue your friend the only way out of the temple is through a very, very dark maze that comes out on the backside of the cliffs. It is said that a giant will be guarding the exit and is not to let anyone out of the maze. If you manage to get past him you will need to head south, through the lava pits of Mercer. There you will need to watch for the deadly lava snakes. If one bites you it won't let go till your blood starts to boil, but by then you're a goner anyway."

Toby shook his head, "Wow!" "it sure doesn't sound very easy."

The old man looked at Toby, "Do you have food and water for three days, maybe four?"

Toby shook his head, "No, I do have food but I don't have any water."

The old man walked over to the wall of the gulch and took a flask that was hanging from an old root sticking out from it. "Here, you can take this. An old lady named Mitizie gave me this for doing something for her. She called it a never ending flask of drinking water. I've used it a few times and it always stays full."

Toby took the flask, "Thank you, but are you sure won't need it?"

"Naw," the old man pointed to somewhere in the dark, "I have two wells over there that give me all the water I can ever use, one has cool water for drinking, the other has warm water for bathing and washing things." The old man threw a mat made from some kind of leaves and grass at Toby's feet, "You can't cross the ice desert at night so you best get some rest, I'll be sure you're awake at sunrise. That way you will be starting out fresh. Always remember, "You will never get to the end of your journey without taking the first step."

Toby thought, "Wow, this guy is full of homespun philosophy." He nodded and smiled, he looked at the mat lying at his feet. It had been a long day and he felt exhausted.

Chapter 6

The First Step

Toby opened his eyes and looked around. He could see the first rays of sunlight creeping over the horizon. He jumped to his feet, grabbed his walking stick, the parcel of food, the bag of phosphorus dust and the flask of water the old man had given him. Then he bent down, neatly rolled up the sleeping mat and leaned it against the wall of the ravine.

"Ha" "I see you're awake and eagre to get started. Did you sleep well?"

Toby jumped a little and turned around, the old man was sitting on a rock, drinking some kind of hot brew that didn't smell very good. Toby nodded, "Yeah, I slept really good last night, guess I was really tired." He pointed to the west where the sun was rising, "It's almost daylight, guess I need to get started, I have a long way to go today. I just hope I don't run into any more wolf looking creatures who want to eat me for dinner."

The old man sat up straight and looked at Toby, "Did you encounter some on your journey here?"

Toby nodded, "Yeah, three of them had me surrounded but I managed to fend them off with my walking stick."

The old man looked shocked, "You beat off three Chisel Toothed Prairie Mongrels with a stick? I don't believe anyone has ever been able to do that before. They always end up being dinner for those vicious curs."

Toby opened his eyes wide, "You called them Chisel Toothed Prairie Mongrels," "is that what they are?"

The old man thought for a moment, "Well, no one really knows what they are or where they came from, they just showed up one day. They have very long chisel like fangs, are very large and strong, and they look to be part wolf and part something else. They always attack in groups of three, usually at night when it hardest to see them. If you were able to take on all three of them at once with just a stick and survive, you may have a chance of rescuing your friend after all. Anyway, you shouldn't need to worry about them, they never venture out to where your heading."

Toby nodded, "good, so all I need to do is get across the ice desert without stepping into quick sand or falling through a thin ice mass." He paused for a moment like he was thinking, "Well, I guess I had better get started," he grinned and waved to the old loner.

The old man nodded, held up a hand and said "Be careful, be safe, and remember, the longest journey always begins with the first step."

Toby nodded again, "Yeah, and here I go," and took a big step forward.

Toby turned east and looked across the ice desert of voo. Off in the distance he could make out the shapes of what looked to be trees. That must be the forest with no name he thought, guess it doesn't look to far, maybe if I'm lucky I can get there by mid-day. Toby half walked, half ran till he came to the edge of the forbidding desert of ice and sand then stopped and looked around. He could make out the faint remains of trails that started from where he was standing. They all led out into the desert but ended abruptly, either at an ice patch or just in the sand. There were also some strange looking foot prints from some kind of animal that seemed to zig-zag in all sorts of directions. Toby stood there for a few minutes leaning on his walking stick, trying to figure out a way to cross this barrier of sand and ice without becoming one of its unsuspecting victims.

Just then he noticed a huge looking rock coming from behind him and slowly moving towards the desert. He watched in amazement as the giant looking boulder came closer, then stopped at the edge of the desert just a few feet from him. The greenish-brown looking oddity seemed to be studying Toby and the harsh terrain ahead. When it was satisfied that the new obstacle standing there posed no danger, the rock looking form started moving forward into the desert. As it passed Toby, he could make out four short legs and a head sticking out from underneath the slow moving creatures back. "Wow!, this must be a turtle of some kind," Toby said out loud. He watched as it lumbered slowly passed him and onto the desert of sand and ice that stretched out ahead of them.

Toby thought for a moment, he figured the turtle must have crossed this dangerous terrain many times and knew a safe way to go. He started following the large reptile staying close behind it. He thought of a story his mother used to tell him, a long time ago, about a tortoise and a hare that ran a race. The tortoise won because the hare got way ahead and stopped to take a nap. The tortoise slowly passed the hare and crossed the finish line while it was still sleeping. Toby smiled, there was no way he wanted to get ahead of this big guy, he felt pretty safe just staying behind going slow. Toby also thought about what the old hermit, or as he wanted to be called, old loner had said. "When the way is slow, the earth will be patient." He smiled and nodded at his thoughts and stayed close behind th slow moving, shell covered oddity.

Toby kept almost bumping into the back side of his reptile guide because it kept stopping and changing directions. Sometimes moving onto an ice field, other times just going around some unseen hazzard in the sand. Toby placed one of his hands on the back of the critter's huge shell and pressed down hard. It seemed not to even notice it. Toby got an idea. He carefully climbed up on the turtle's back, then leaned back and got comfortable. "Ha" he quietly said out loud, "I'll just relax and let someone else do the driving." He had heard that from a car commercial on TV. Toby nodded off a couple of times, almost falling off once. That woke him up quick. After that he sat up straight on the turtles back an watched as the trees of the forest with no name grew taller as they got closer. Toby looked back in the direction they had came, it looked like they had come about two/thirds of the way.

Suddenly the turtle came to a full stop. It stretched its long neck and head as far out from under it shell as it could and looked around. Then it raised its head and looked straight back at the uninvited rider on its back. Toby felt uneasy about hitching a ride on the gentle reptiles back and slid off. He figured he would just follow along behind it again like before.

The giant reptile had different ideas. It pulled its head back into its shell and started throwing sand up on its back with its huge feet. They looked big and flat like boat oars with claws. Toby stood back and watched in amazement as the tortoise piled sand half way up its back. Then pulled its feet back under the sand and into its shell. Toby remembered seeing a documentary on T V about huge snapping turtles, this was how they rested. They would bury themselves partly in sand leaving only their armor like shells exposed. This way they didn't need to worry about predators trying to feast on them while they slept.

Toby wondered how long his reptile guide was going to rest. He needed to get out of the desert quickly and to the other side of the forest as soon as possible. He needed to be at the stone towers of Essor before sunset. Rain was depending on him to save her and he couldn't let her down. He looked at the trees on the edge of the desert, there was still quite a way to go to reach them and the forest with no name. He wondered how did the tortoise manage to navigate the treacherous terrain they had crossed. It seemed to know exactly when to stop, turn or even back up a few times. He also kept thinking about the old hermits saying, "When the way is slow, the earth is patient." Toby thought out loud, "The turtle walks on all four legs, not just two." "That's it." "When you are walking on four legs, if one of the front ones steps in quick sand or breaks through the ice, the other three still have control over you, keeping you from falling through the ice or getting pulled into quick sand. Then you simply back up a little and go around the hazzard."

Toby dropped down on his hands and knees, looked around as if to see if anyone was watching, then said out loud, "Well' if I'm going to get out of here I guess I'll have to crawl the rest of the way like a little kid," then he slowly started crawling towards the trees off in the distance.

Chapter 7

Into The Forest

Toby stood up and looked back at the vast expanse of wasteland he had managed to cross. He was glad to be out of the sand, ice fields and dry dead brush that dotted the landscape. He bent down to brush off his pant legs and realized that his hands and knees were raw and bleeding from crawling for so long. He looked at his watch, it was almost two o-clock. That only gave him about four hours to get through the forest and to the two stone pillars of Essor before sunset. The old hermit had said there was a pathway heading north through the forest, and also not to stop and smell the flowers along the way because they could devour you. Then Toby said out loud as though he was talking to someone, "Don't need to worry about that, I don't have time to be dilly-dallying around checking out the different plants today, I've got a long way to go and a short time to get there." Toby took a big drink from the flask the old hermit had given him, adjusted his pouch of dust and bag of food that hung over his shoulders, took a firm grip on his walking stick and headed into the dense array of trees and shrubs.

He thought about the flask of water the old hermit had given him and had said that an old lady named Mitizie had put a magical spell on it so it would never go dry. He remembered the story that Lady Zelda had told him about the twelve witches and one warlock coming to this land. The warlock was named Dr. Zodd, and one of the witches was called Mystic Mitizie. Could she have been the same woman who gave the flask to the hermit? Maybe there really are witches living here, after all, he had taken several drinks from it and it was still full. He shrugged his shoulders and started to walk a little faster.

Toby's thoughts shifted to Rain who was being held in the lost temple and was to be sacrificed tomorrow night. He could almost feel her trembling with fear and hoping her friend would be in time to save her. The thought of someone doing this to his best friend made him angry. He hoped someday he would meet Dr. Zodd face to face and somehow make him regret his evil actions.

Toby stopped briefly for a moment to get some dried meat and a biscuit from his bag of food. He hadn't eaten all day and was getting hungry. He sat down on a patch of grass, laid his walking stick beside hin and took a bite of the jerky. He sat there chewing on his food and looking up at the sun through the dense trees when he realized something was tangled around his ankle. He jerked his leg up to free it but it got tighter and started to pull him towards some strange looking plants on the side of the trail. He grabbed for his walking stick but couldn't quite reach it. He tried to hold onto the long grass but the tentacle like growth was very strong and kept pulling him towards a giant, cannibalistic looking flower that was slowly opening up showing thousands of sharp thorns on its inside. Toby remembered the old hermit saying they would pull you inside, close up around you crushing you and eventually devouring you.

No matter how hard Toby struggled to free himself he was unable to get away from the green tentacle that kept dragging him closer and closer to a certain horrific death. He felt helpless and weak from fear, closed his eyes dreading the fate that awaited him. Then, suddenly he could hear Rains voice in his head,

"Toby, use the knife, use the knife I gave you."

Toby reached down to his pant's pocket and could feel the knife. He pulled it out and opened the longest blade, it was still razor sharp. He sat up, bent over and started hacking at the long slim tentacle wrapped around his ankle. After several chops the long thin plant that held his leg was cut through freeing him. He jumped up, hustled over to his walking stick, grabbed it and started down the trail as quick as he could, being careful where he stepped, leaving the giant, man eating fly trap behind him.

He thought about hearing Rain's voice telling him to use the knife which saved him from who knows what. He shrugged his shoulders, "Maybe this telepathic communication isn't so bad after all." Then he started wondering what he would do if he made it to the temple in time to rescue Rain. "If a simple flower almost devoured him, how would he be able to cope with a living stone monster lurking somewhere in the dark maze, looking forward to its annual meal?

Again he heard Rains voice in his head, "Don't worry about it, I'm sure you will figure something out when you get here. You just need to stop dilly-dallying around." Her telepathic voice tried to sound cheerful but it was shaking with fear.

Toby answered back out loud, "Don't worry, I'm not stopping for any more picnics, and I will be there with time to spare." He was trying to reassure her and cheer her up.

After an another hour of brisk walking Toby could see the end of the trail and the edge of the forest with no name. He thought "If I could name this forest I would call it Nightmare Forest." He hustled past the last few trees and bushes at the edge then stopped to look back at the peaceful looking pathway. "What a deceiving place" he thought, "all the tall shady trees and grassy areas around them make it look really inviting, but then there's those giant pink and red man eating plants that hope someone stops there to have a picnic so they can also have one."

He turned and looked to the north. He could see the two stone towers of Essor off in the distance. He took a quick drink from his flask and headed towards them. There was no pathway or trail to follow so he had to carefully pick his way, avoiding rocks, cactus, and some rather large, yellow and brown snakes laying in the sun. As he got nearer to the stone towers he could make out the red jagged cliffs of Morax raising up majesticially behind them.

Toby stopped and rested on his walking stick for a moment. Suddenly he was feeling extremely tired and afraid. The day of crossing the ice desert and his experience in the evil forest with no name had been very stressful. He wondered what he had gotten himself into. He, was somewhere out in the middle of nowhere, trying to rescue a girl from some hideous monster in a temple that no one even knew where it was. Then his thoughts turned to Rain again, she had to be scared to death, being held somewhere in a dark maze, waiting to be sacrificed to some dreadful creature created by an evil wizard, and her only hope of being saved was by him. Toby stood up straight, squared his shoulders and started towards the two stone towers again. "Quit feeling sorry for yourself and act like a man" he said out loud.

Chapter 8

Ashpit Ashley

As Toby got closer to the giant rock towers he noticed a very large bird fly from the top of one of the columns and was circling high over head. He didn't give it much thought, he was concentrating on reaching the towers before sunset so he could see their shadows on the red looking cliffs behind them. There were several large pieces of rock scattered between the two columns that had probably broken away from the tops and fell to their resting places.

He paused for a moment, resting on his walking stick, while looking for a good spot to wait for the sun to set. Suddenly, without warning, a large shadow passed over his head and there was a loud screeching "Caaaaaw" and the whooshing sound of flapping wings coming from behind him. He spun around just in time to see the huge flying oddity diving straight for him, its huge dark colored beak wide opened and the talons on its scaly feet extended out ready to grab its prey. Toby dove face first into the dirt just in time to avoid being a victim for the huge flying menace.

He watched as the giant, reptile looking creature started to circle around to make another pass at its intended meal. Toby knew he had to do something and do it fast. He jumped up to his feet and made a beeline for the closest pile of rocks he could hide in. He jumped between two of them just in time to avoid the flying reptiles second pass. Again he watched as it started to circle around for a third try.

Toby thought for a moment, he knew that bats flew in the dark using something like sonar to guide them. They would zero in on a flying insect or something and follow it tell they caught it. Off to Toby's right was a piece of rock sticking out of the ground. It was about a foot across and almost as tall as he was. He jumped up, ran over and stood as close as he could to it. He hoped this flying reptile used sonar like bats did to follow its prey and wouldn't be aware of the rock column he was covering. He heard the loud "Caaaw" again and watched as the winged serpent came straight at him. He started to tremble as he stood directly in the path of the diving creature, hoping his plan would work. When the creature was almost on top of him he dove to the side of the rock, landing face first, flat on the ground.

The huge flying menace tried to miss the rock column but one of it's giant wings hit it hard and made a satisfying "Splat." Toby watched as the wounded predator struggled to fly away.

"Very good, very, very good" an old woman's voice called out. "You certainly foiled its dinner plans for today."

Toby spun around, he was still shaking from his close encounter with the flying reptile and thought maybe he only imagined hearing an old woman's voice way out here in no-mans land. The voice called out again,

"I'm over here."

Toby watched in amazement as an old woman slowly emerged from behind sone jagged looking rocks.

"I didn't mean to startle you, but I was keeping out of sight from that flying monstrosity. Its been a pest around here for quite some time now. Maybe since you gave it a taste of the rock it will think twice before coming back. Anyway, whoever you are, you're just in time for dinner. I was out gathering some wild herbs when I spotted you playing "Come and get me" with that winged menace".

Toby watched the old woman as she walked out from the large rocks she had been hiding behind. She was dressed funny, wearing a red and green bonnet with a strap that tied under her chin, a long grey and white dress that came to the ground and a white apron that was tied around her waist in a neat bow. She was not very tall and looked happy to see someone.

She made a motion with her hand, "Come on over and sit down for a moment, you won't need to worry about your flying friend coming back, by now it's probably someplace pouting over its busted wing."

Toby laughed a little, she was kind of funny in her own way. He nodded, walked over to the woman and sat on a rock across from her. He kept his walking stick close at his side just in case he needed it for something more than just talking.

The old woman spoke first, "You are a fine looking young man, What is your name?"

"Toby, Toby Tuttles and I came from Duppland, and what is your name?"

"Ashley, but where I come from they refer to me as "Ashpit Ashley.""

Toby nodded, "Do you live out here all alone, and why do they call you that, does anyone else live out here?"

The old woman laughed, "Boy, you're full of all kinds of questions aren't you. Come on and have some dinner with me and I will be happy to answer all of them."

She stood up and headed back towards the two large rocks she had been hiding behind. Toby stood up and followed. He could smell something cooking like roasted meat of some kind. It smelled really good and he realized he was really hungry. They passed between the two rocks and into a small courtyard where there was a table and benches all carved from stone. On the far side of the courtyard was a small hogan type hut with a door and two windows visible. She motioned for Toby to sit down, and disappeared into the hut. After a couple of moments she reappeared with a large trey of food and a couple of large blue napkins. She sat the trey down, handed Toby a napkin and motioned to a fountain at the far side of the courtyard. There was water tumbling gently down two small waterfalls, into a little pond and then disappearing out behind the hogan in a small clear stream.

"You can wash up over there before eating, your hands and face are a mess."

"Yes ma'am" Toby said with a grin, she sounded just like his mother did sometimes.

He dried his face and hands with the napkin and sat back down. The woman nodded, "There, now you look much better." She sat a stone plate in front of him with a large portion of meat and some sort of vegetables on it.

"Now I will answer all your questions. Yes, I live out here all alone, no, I don't know of anyone else living in these parts. I was self-exiled from my group shortly after we arrived in this land. It does get lonely out here and it's nice to see a stranger once in a while to talk to and share a meal with."

Toby nodded, "Why were you exiled? Did you break some law or something like that?"

She smiled, "Well, something like that, I was the seamstress for a Dr. Zodd who was the head of our group. I always made his clothes to his specifications and only in black. For some reason black was the only color he would wear. Then one day I came across a beautiful piece of a bluish purple satin looking material that was amazing to look at and was very strong. I figured I would surprise the Dr. and made him a beautiful cape out of this one of a kind fabric. He looked at it, threw it in my face, and screamed" "GET THIS PIECE OF TRASH OUT OF MY SIGHT AND DON'T EVER, EVER BRING ME ANYTHING LIKE THIS AGAIN." "I grabbed the cape and ran away from him as fast as I could. I went straight to his bed chambers, gathered all the clothes I had made for him, carried them out to a fire pit and tossed them into the flames. I picked up a long stick and stirred the ashes till every bit of clothing was gone. The only thing I saved was the cape I had worked so hard on. That's when all the other women in the compound started calling me Ashpit Ashley, and that's when and I decided I needed to leave."

"There was a small tree growing just outside the compound with a fence around it. It was called the tree of life because it was believed that if you drank tea made from its leaves it would slow down the ageing process. One night when it was really dark I wrapped all my belongings in the cape and snuck out of the compound. On the way out I cut a small branch from the sacred tree when no one was looking and figured I would start a new one someplace. I finally ended up here where there is plenty of water and game, and the soil is very rich and plants do very well."

Toby finished his dinner, wiped his hands on his pants legs, which got him a unpleasant look from his host, then stood up and looked back at the two towers. The sun was starting to go down below the horizon and the two long shadows from the towers were right at the base of the red stone cliffs.

"Now it's my turn to ask the questions" the old woman said in a serious voice. "Why are you out here all by yourself, and just what are you looking for?"

Toby sat back down, "Well there is supposed to be a temple somewhere hidden in those red cliffs and I need to find it by tomorrow."

The old woman narrowed her eyes, "You don't mean Dr. Zodd's hidden temple, you need to stay away from that place, its evil and dangerous. Why would you even think about going there?"

Toby stood up again, shoved his hands in his pockets, "A very good friend of mine has been taken there and is to be sacrificed to some sort of monster tomorrow night. I am trying to rescue her before that happens. I was told I might find the entrance in those cliffs somewhere between the shadows of those two stone towers. Do you know anything about it?"

The woman looked at Toby for a moment, "Is this person your girl friend?"

Toby shook his head, "No, no, of course not, she's just a very good friend."

The woman smiled, "Soooo, She's a very good friend and she is obviously a girl."

"Yeah, something like that" Toby muttered.

"Well, it's very gallant of you to risk everything to rescue your friend."

Toby looked at the old woman, "Since you used to work for the Dr., do you know where the temple is? I would appreciate it if you could tell me."

"I have never been there, I do know that he was building it somewhere about half way up the side of the cliffs between the shadows of the towers. It is rumored that there is a hidden stairway behind a giant slab of rock, a fission that broke away from the cliff and stands upright along side of them. It makes it almost impossible to see the stairs unless you know exactly where to look. It is said that the stairs and entrance to the temple are hidden between the rock slab and the cliffs. I will point it out to you tomorrow at sunrise. "I do know this," the old woman continued, "It is very dangerous just going into the temple. Once you enter the chambers the only way out is through a very long, pitch black maze with miles of dead end passages. And to make things worse, there is no way to get past some evil living stone monster that Dr. Zodd created. It comes to life once every year about now, and roams the passageways looking for a sacrifice promised to it by the Dr. It can see in the dark and lurks somewhere in the passageways, devouring anything that it can find. If you do manage to get past it, there is an exit that comes out on the back side of the cliffs but it is guarded by a giant named Gort. The Dr. Has instructed him not to let anyone out of the maze."

Toby listened intently to the old woman, she seemed to know more about the temple than anyone so far. He turned and looked at the cliffs that were slowly fading from sight as the daylight turned to darkness.

"It sounds very risky but my friend is depending on me and I can't let her down. I have to try to save her."

The old woman shook her head, "Even if you find her you will need to get past the monster and the giant guard outside the exit, and that's almost impossible. The monster sees very well in the dark maze, but you won't. Once you enter the maze it is so dark in there that you won't even be able to see your hand when it's in front of your face. And remember the giant guard, no one can get past him. Dr. Zodd is a very, very evil man and has created a very evil place."

Toby looked up at the woman, "You said you worked for him when he came to this land over three hundred years ago, yet he is still alive and you don't look very old either, how is that possible?"

The woman smiled, "Well thank you" "As I told you earlier, when we entered this land, Dr. Zodd discovered a tree and called it the tree of life. If you were to drink tea made from its leaves it would greatly slow the ageing process. The tree was well guarded and only a select few were given the leaves to make the tea. I was one of them and found the brew to be quite tasty.

I didn't know at that time if it really did slow the aging process but since I enjoyed drinking it I took a small branch from the tree when I left the compound. I wandered around the countryside till I ended up here and have been here ever since. I planted the tiny branch beside the spring back in those rocks," she pointed somewhere behind her hut, "and started a tree of my own. It has done quite well and I enjoy having a cup of the tea every so often."

"Wow, when I start talking I just go on and on," she placed her hand on her chest, "Anyway, now you know the story of my life since I came to this land with Dr. Zodd and eleven other women. I now know that most of the other women have left him because of his wicked ways. He has had over three hundred years to develop many strange and evil powers that he uses to control people and other things that he chooses. Well, I hope I haven't bored you."

Toby shook his head, "oh no ma'am," "It has been very interesting."

The woman walked behind a large rock and came back with something under her arm, "Well I can't stop you from looking for the temple and I won't try. I admire your courage so I'm going to give you something to take with you. I see your not carrying a coat or wrap of any kind and It does get quite cold here in the north country at night so I want you to have this. It will protect you and keep you quite comfortable," she handed him the beautiful bluish-purple cape she had made over three hundred years ago.

Toby held it up, "Wow, this is beautiful, really beautiful."

The woman pointed to a pile of leaves and straw, "You need to get some rest, you would never be able to find the stairway to the temple in the dark, and you will have a long day tomorrow. You can leave at first light, and before you go I will point out the location where the hidden stairway is believed to be."

Toby nodded, he'd had a very long day, was tired and quite scared. He laid down on the makeshift bed, his walking stick close beside him and covered himself with his new cape. His thoughts shifted to Rain. In his mind he could see her tied by her hands to a iron ring over her head.

She looked at him and said, ":Please be careful but hurry, I'm really scared."

Toby mumbled softly, "I'll be there tomorrow I promise." Then he closed his eyes and was immediately asleep.

Chapter 9

The Red Cliffs Of Morax

Toby awoke to the smell of something good. He got to his feet, brushed off some dry leaves and straw from his jeans and slipped on his sneakers.

"Oh good, you're awake." The old woman walked over to Toby, "Here, take these," she handed him a small cloth parcel, they will give you energy and keep you alert."

Toby looked at the parcel, "What are they?"

"Oh, just some cookies I made." She pointed behind her, I have a small garden out back where I can grow the things necessary to make them. I'd like to show you around a little more but you look anxious to be on your way. I told you last night I'd show you how to find the hidden stairway that goes up the side of the cliffs to the temple entrance."

Toby nodded, "If you can do that it would be a big help."

The old woman walked over beside him and pointed with a long thin finger. "Can you see that jagged line starting at the base of the cliffs and running diagonally up the side."

Toby nodded, "Yeah, it looks like some sort of crack going up the face of the cliff."

"Well," the old lady paused, "It's not a crack, it's part of the face of the cliff that broke away hundreds of years ago and landed upright just far enough away to be able to hide a stairway behind it. It's only visible when the early morning sunlight makes a shadow behind it. You won't be able to see it when the sun gets a little higher because the shadow goes away and it just looks like part of the cliff. So you'll need to get a good fix on it while it's visible."

"Yes ma'am, thank you very much," Toby shook her hand, "I have enjoyed my short stay and hope someday we will meet again."

She nodded, "I'm sure we will, yes, I'm sure we will."

Toby threw the cape over his shoulders, "By the way, thanks again for this, it's quite warm and you're right, it is a little cool this morning."

"Oh you're quite welcome, I'm just glad that after all these years I could give to someone who would appreciate it."

Toby smiled, waved goodby and started towards the faint jagged line that was barely visible on the face of the cliffs. He had to pick his way carefully, not to trip over any of the sharp rocks or get caught up in the razor sharp thorns from one of the many cactus that seemed to grow everywhere. His thoughts kept going back to the old woman who had been so nice to him. She was dressed so neatly in new clothes that she certainly made for herself, probably using fabric woven from hemp and cotton like plants growing somewhere in the area. He looked at the new cape he was wearing, the bluish purple cloth looked almost metallic in the morning sun. She said it would keep him warm and protect him, and he couldn't forget her saying that she was sure they would meet again, why would she say that?

From time to time he would look at the dark reddish cliffs and at an old dead tree that he could see just to the left of where the hidden stairway was supposed to be. As he got nearer to the cliffs they looked very majestic and forbidding, making him feel very meek, small and scared.

He turned his thoughts to Rain. He could see her in his mind. She was cold, frightened and sobbing. Her telepathic ability to communicate with him grew stronger and more clear as he got closer to where she was being held a prisoner. Toby said out loud, "I'm almost there, I've got food and something to get you warm, I'm just about to the entrance of the temple."

"I have faith in you, just be careful," Her voice was so clear it was almost as if she was standing next to him.

Tears came to Toby's eyes, The thought of his friend being tied up somewhere in a dark dungeon, cold and afraid with him being her only hope of survival made him forget his fears of being alone in a strange and hostile land. He started walking faster, the sharp rocks tearing at his sneakers and cactus thorns poking through his trouser legs, pricking the tender skin inside. He paid little attention to these hazzards and concentrated only on the cliffs that loomed high overhead. He kept watching the old dead tree at the base of them that he was using as a marker. It looked to be only a few hundred yards away.

He froze in his footsteps as a large shadow passed over his head. He looked up and saw another of the huge, flying reptile like creatures circling above him. It seemed to waiting for him to get to an open area where it could swoop down and grab him with its hook like talons and carry him off to some distant location to feast on.

Toby quickly ducked between a couple of large rocks and squatted down so that the flying menace couldn't get to him. He hoped maybe this flying nightmare would go away soon so that he could get to the cliffs and find the stairway, but it wasn't leaving. It continued to circle overhead, patiently waiting for its prey to move out into the open. Toby realized he couldn't wait it out, it probably could fly in circles for hours without getting tired. The updrafts from the face of the cliffs could keep it aloft all day with it only having to use its wings ever so often to change directions.

Toby could feel the grey cloak of fear closing in on him. It seemed like everything in this strange country was out to get him. The chisel toothed mongrols, the ice desert, man eating flowers, and now flying dinosaurs. He could feel tears coming to his eyes and he was shaking with fear.

"Stop that, You mustn't give up that easy." It was Rains voice again, she sounded desperate.

Toby shook his head trying to get his composure back. He Thought, "With her telepathic ability I can't even feel sorry for myself without her knowing it.

"That's right" it was her voice again, "Now, listen to me, you need to find a long stick and sharpen one end of it with the knife I gave you, then you need to shove it down that old buzzards craw when it comes at you. I know you can do it so please hurry."

Toby nodded as though she was standing there beside him. He felt a little ashamed, cowering down between a couple of rocks feeling sorry for himself when she was depending on him to rescue her.

Toby looked up at the flying reptile. It was circling lower now, probably planning a late breakfast or early lunch. Toby raised his arm and shook his fist at the creature, calling it a few unkind words. This short outburst seemed to give hin some renewed courage. He looked down at the cape the old woman had given him, it was shining in the sunlight. He was hoping she actually was a witch an had sewn some magical powers in it. She did say it would keep him warm and protect him. He pulled it up over his shoulders and said out loud.

"I don't feel any protection here, maybe it will just keep me from getting sunburned." He reached into his front pocket and pulled out the knife Rain had given him, "She's right, I'll need to stop this flying nightmare on my own." He looked around for a long tree branch, there was one about thirty or forty yards away laying out in the open with no rocks or other cover to hide behind when he reached it. He would have to run over, grab it, and get back to the rocks before the flying nightmare could get to him. He removed the straps holding his food, water and phosphorus dust and laid them next to his walking stick. He waited till it pasted over him and was heading away to circle again. He hoped it wouldn't be able to see him till it was coming back around, giving him time to grab the dead branch and get back to his cover.

The predator passed over where Toby was crouching and when it was going away he jumped up like a sprint runner and shot forward with speed he never knew he had. His feet were just a blur and the silvery cape stood out behind him like the pictures he had seen of flying super heros. Toby grabbed the branch and was back to his cover before the flying critter realized what had happened. He squatted down, panting a little, took the edge of the cape and looked at it.

"Wow, maybe this thing does have some magic in it, I've never been able to run that fast before." He picked up his knife and started to sharpen the end of the branch. The wood was hard but the knife was sharp and cut through it without too much effort. Toby kept a watch on the unwanted winged oddity circling over him. Each time it came around it seemed to be a little lower. After several minutes the wooden shaft had a fine tapered point on one end. Toby carefully folded the blade into the knife and slid it back into his pocket.

He sat for a couple of minutes with his back against a rock, wondering what chance he would have of warding off this giant menace with only a pointed stick. If he failed it would probably be the end for him and for Rain. If he simply just sat there cowering down till dark waiting for this thing to go roost somewhere, if that's what they do, then it would be to late to rescue Rain and save her from the hideous monster.

Again, Toby could feel the blanket of fear coming over him. He again thought about Rain, waiting in some dark, cold, stone passageway, hoping he would be able to rescue her. He felt confused and scared, very scared.

"It's O K Toby" It was rains voice in his head again, "I know how hard this must be for you. It looks like Dr Zodd may have beaten us both. If you want to turn around and go back I wouldn't blame you. I'm sorry I got you into this mess."

Toby raised his head, looked towards the red cliffs and said out loud, "I'm not quitting, I might be tired and a little scared, but I'm coming to get you. There's no way the evil Dr Zodd can beat the two of us. Now just relax while I take care of this ugly creature that's been annoying me for the last hour."

Toby was embarrassed and ashamed that Rain thought he was a coward and a quitter. He looked up just in time to see the flying serpent pass just over his head and start to circle around again. Toby slowly rose to his feet, knees shaking and his teeth chattering. "Well here goes nothing" he said out loud, and with his long pointed stick over his shoulder he walked out into a clearing and stood up straight so that his adversary would have an easy target. The flying creature came around and could see its intended victim just standing there. It was flying so low that every time it flapped its huge wings dust and bits of dry grass would be blown off the ground. Now it was coming straight at him, the claws on its ugly scaley feet extended and its large beak opened wide, as though it wanted to grab and devour him, all at the same time. Toby drew the makeshift lance from his shoulder, tucked it under his arm and gripped it as tight as he could with both hands. He braced one foot on a rock behind him, and stood there, his cape flapping in the breeze, and his lance pointed directly at the charging enemy

"Caaaaw," the creature let out a loud, blood curdling, half screech, half roar as it prepared to attack its prey. Toby braced himself and pointed his lance directly at the wide opened mouth rushing at him. He knew if he missed his target it would probably rip him in two. He closed his eyes tightly, clenched his teeth and waited, not sure how this nightmare was going to end.

There was a powerful blow that sent him airborne and backwards several feet, landing flat on his back in a pile of weeds and rocks. He opened his eyes and looked up. The huge critter was flying away very awkwardly. It was shaking its head back and forth vigorously, trying to rid itself of the wooden lance that stuck out of its craw. Toby stood up, brushed himself off, and watched as the wounded menace disappeared from sight, then said out loud, more for Rains benefit than his, "Well, I guess that wasn't so bad, was it?" He grabbed his water flask, bag of phosphorus dust, his food and the cookies the old lady had given him, slung them over his shoulder and with his walking stick started out again.

Chapter 10

The Stone Door

It was almost noon when Toby got to the base of the cliffs. He stopped, opened the parcel of cookies, selected the largest one then neatly folded the napkin back around the rest, and took a bite. It tasted really good, kind of like peanut butter and chocolate. He slowly finished the cookie, enjoying every bite down to the last crumb, then took a long drink from his water flack and looked around.

Now he needed to find the stairway to the temple door, and somehow get to Rain before the evil stone monster devoured her. He shook his head, grabbed his walking stick and headed in the direction the old woman had pointed out earlier that morning. He looked up at the shear walls of the cliffs, they were very high and a dull reddish-brown color. There were several cracks and crevices in them that could hide the fabled stairway from view. Along the base there were several large rocks that had probably fallen from somewhere high above and were resting peacefully where they had landed. A few had lizards lazily sunning themselves on them, enjoying the midday warmth.

About a hundred yards from where he stood he could see a large section of the cliff that had broken away from the face and was standing upright about three or four feet from it. As Toby got nearer to the passageway between the cliff and the wall he could make out the faint outline of what appeared to be stairs going up the side of the cliff behind the wall, well hidden from view.

"Ha," he said out loud, "the old woman was right." He glanced down at his watch, it was almost twelve-thirty, he needed to hurry. When he got to the stone stairway he looked up and gasped, it was the longest stairway he had ever seen, and to make it worse, the first several steps were covered with snakes, laying there sunning themselves. Toby had never feared snakes, he had a couple for pets back home. He fed them insects, small rodents, and gave them small amounts of water. He had learned from watching the nature channel on TV that most snakes would not strike unless they felt threatened. He hoped that would be the same in this land of horrors and weird oddities.

He held his walking stick high so it wouldn't clatter on the stone stairs and slowly started up. He carefully placed his foot softly on each step as he went, hoping not to waken or frighten any of the sleeping serpents. Finally, after what seemed like hours, the steps ahead looked to be clear of the legless reptiles. Toby let out a sigh of relief and started to climb faster, hoping to make up some of the time he lost getting past the hundreds of snakes behind him.

He looked up and could see what looked to be the top of the stairway but there was no sign of a temple door nor any opening leading into the stone cliff. He hoped the trek up this long, long stairway wouldn't have been for nothing. He had no desire to go back down through all those ugly snakes again. Finally he reached the top and stood on a long flat stone landing. He paused, took a drink from his flask and looked around. The landing was quite long and faded into the cliff making the only way down the same long stairway he had come up. He slowly started walking, looking up and down the stone wall of the cliff for a hidden door or passageway.

He paused for a moment, right beside him, almost covered with vines and shrubs growing out the side of the cliff were two upright stone columns with a large flat stone resting on top of them. Between then was a large flat stone that looked to be a door, but there was no handle, latch or visible hinges. Toby wondered if the opening had been sealed so that no one could enter it. He tried pushing on one side of the stone slab as hard as he could with both hands but it wouldn't budge. He tried pushing on the other side and thought he felt it move just a little. He took a deep breath and pushed as hard as he could. The huge door slowly swung open making ghostly sounds like two stones being scraped together.

Chapter 11

Enter The Chamber

Toby brushed aside an array of cobwebs and slowly walked through the partly opened stone door, then stood there in amazement. He was in a very large chamber with lighted torches hanging from the walls on each end. There was a very large heavy wooden table in the center with one chair behind it and three on the front side. In the stone wall behind the table were three thick wooden doors. Each was attached to the wall by massive iron hinges and there were locks that slid into holes cut into the stone wall so that no one could open them from the other side if the door was closed and locked. Toby brushes the array of cobwebs from his face and hair that he had walked through and hoped he wasn't covered with spiders. He looked at the burning torches and called out in a soft voice, "Hello, Hello, is anyone here." There was no answer, just the hollow sound of his voice in the large open chamber.

Then he heard a quiet thud behind him. Toby slowly turned around and looked at the heavy stone door that he had left opened. It was now closed tightly. There were no handles, knobs nor anything else to pull it open with from inside. Attached to the top of it were two strong iron chains that went over a rounded stone column and down through the stone floor. Toby figured one was attached to a weight to offset the weight of the heavy stone door so it could be opened, and the second to a heavier counterweight that would pull the door closed after it was opened. There were four large iron hinges that attached the door securely to the stone wall much like the pictures of old dungeons he had seen. Toby thought, "No wonder Ashpit Ashley said that once you entered the temple, the only was out was through the maze."

He walked over to one of the burning torches and wondered why they were lit if there was no one there. Then he noticed something dripping into the bowl of the torch from where the flame was burning. Above each torch there was a spout coming out from the temple's stone walls with drops of oil falling from it into the torches basin. Toby shook his head in amazement, the torches had probably been burning for over three hundred years, and would continue to do so till the supply of oil was stopped. He figured there must be a natural supply of it from somewhere inside the massive stone walls of the cliff that fed the flames. Their dim, flickering yellowish glow danced eerily on the grey stone walls making the chamber seem haunted and uninviting.

He slowly walked over to the door on one side of the room and cautiously pushed it opened. There was a long narrow room with some sort of alter on one end. There were three stone benches facing it and behind it stood a large statue of a thin man with a short beard, wearing a cape with a pointed hood. Toby reached down and felt the cape he was wearing, it looked a lot like the one on the statue. Behind the statue was a long thin table with three urns on one side and a half burnt candle on the other. In the rear of the room was another burning torch, fed by the natural oil that dripped from the wall. Toby said softly out loud, "Looks like a chamber of horrors," then slowly backed out of the room and turned towards the door on the far side of the chamber. He walked cautiously holding his walking stick out in front of him with both hands as if to ward off any unseen entities lurking in the dimly lit room.

The door was partly ajar. Toby slowly pushed it the rest of the way open. In the middle of the room was a large flat stone fixture with an old pad or mattress on it. It must have been used for a bed. Toby thought, "This is where the Emerald Princess was probably held captive waiting for her dreadful wedding day." There were no torches burning in this room and the back of it was dark. Toby thought he could make out the forms of some large vases and a seat of some kind against the back wall. He shook his head, left the cold room and looked at the door in the middle of the long wall. It was closed tightly. Toby said out loud, hoping to calm his nerves a little, "That must be the dreaded door to the maze, well here goes nothing," Hearing himself talking out loud didn't help much, his knees were still shaking and his teeth chattering.

He slowly walked up to the heavy wooden door. It to was fastened to the wall by massive iron hinges on one side, a large handle on the other side to pull it open, and a latch that would drop into place locking it when it was closed so it couldn't be pushed open from the other side. He gulped, this had to be the door leading into the maze where Rain and the dreaded stone monster would be. He hoped Rain was all right, she hadn't been on his mind for a while and he hoped she was just sleeping.

He slowly pushed the door opened and stepped into a dim hallway that went for a short distance then turned into a very dark corridor. Toby paused for a moment wondering if he should continue, or go back and try to find a torch or something to light the way. It didn't take long for the decision to be made for him, he heard the door close behind him and the latch drop into place. Now he was in total darkness and the only way out was through the maze. He started slowly walking in the darkness using his walking stick like a probe, tapping the stone walls on both sides of him and feeling the floor ahead for rocks or holes. He tried to look back but there was no way to tell where he was or how far he had come, all he could see was the blackness of the maze. He looked at his watch, the phosphorus hands showed three-twenty. This gave Toby an idea. He opened his bag of phosphorus dust and dropped a pinch of it on the floor. It made a small yellowish-green glow that slightly lit up the wall next to it. Toby figured that he would use his walking stick as a probe and drop a pinch of dust every fifteen or twenty steps. That way he could always look back and see the way he had come, and if he ran into a dead end it would be easier go back and find another passageway. He reached down and touched his cape. Somehow now it was making him feel brave and adventurous without any fear. Again he thought about what the old woman had said when she gave it to him, "It will keep you safe and warm."

Toby started out again, using his walking stick as a probe in the total darkness, tapping both sides of the narrow passageway and the floor in front of him. He felt like a blind man using a long white cane. Slowly, step by step he made his way into the sea of blackness ahead, Occasionally he would come to a dead end and have to go back to find another passage leading from the one he was in.

After what seemed like hours of stumbling through the dark maze of passageways that seemed to lead to nowhere Toby stopped. There was a large opening in the wall to his right. He took a drink from his flask, looked back in the direction he had come, dropped two pinches of phosphorus dust marking a turn and ventured into the new passageway. As he walked he noticed the floor seemed to be going downhill. After a few steps it started getting really steep. He would touch the floor with his staff two or three times before each step to be sure it was safe.

Suddenly, without any warning, Toby's feet slid out from underneath him and he fell backwards, hard on his backside. He tried to get up but there was something wet and slick on the floor. Each time he tried to stand up his feet would slide out from underneath him and he would slip farther down the slanting floor. Then he started sliding, slow at first but as the floor got steeper he started going faster, much faster.

Finally Toby came to a stop against a stone wall at the bottom of the incline. He sat up and looked around but all he could see was blackness. His hands and arms felt like they had oil on them from the slick floor. Toby thought that it was probably from the same source of oil that fed the torches in the main chamber. He shrugged, grabbed his staff, stood up and let out a loud moan. His rear was really hurting from falling on it when he slipped on the oily floor and he could feel a knot on the back of his head.

Chapter 12

Thunder In The Dark

"**T**oby, Toby, is that you?"

Toby peered into the darkness towards where the loud whisper came from. "Yeah, it's me, but is that really you or just your telepathic voice I'm hearing"

"It's really me, you dummy, I think I'm just a few feet from you. I'm tied to a iron ring coming out of the wall over my head. If you work your way along the wall you shouldn't have to come very far to get to me, and keep your voice down." Toby touched the wall with his walking stick, the passageway was wide and only went one direction from where his fall and all the sliding had landed him.

"O-K, I'm against the wall and coming your way as quiet as I can."

"OUCH," she whispered, "why are you jabbing me with a stick?"

Toby grinned a little, "Oops, sorry, just trying to be careful."

"Well, you need to be more careful than that, now find my hands and get me untied."

Toby groped the wall in the darkness till he touched a cold bare arm, he worked his way up and felt her hands tied to the wall. He pulled out his pocket knife and whispered, "I'm going to cut you lose, and I'll be very careful." Toby slowly and carefully cut the ropes holding her hands. Rain lowered her arms and touched Toby's hand, she was sobbing.

"Oh Toby, Toby," "I knew you would come for me. I knew that no one in Duppland would be smart enough or have the courage to find me. But now look at the fix I've gotten you into."

Toby patted her hand, "Don't cry, everything is going to be okay."

Rain swallowed hard, "I'm not so sure, It may already be too late. I've heard noises and weird howls coming from somewhere in the maze." "This must be the night of the full moon bringing the minotaur to life."

Toby thought for a moment, Rain had stopped sobbing which made him feel easier. "We can't go back the way I came because there is a very steep incline with oil on it that you can't climb up. We'll need to sneak past the monster and try to find our way out the back entrance."

Rain sniffed a couple of times, "That may be harder than you think, that stone creep can see in the dark, and I can't even see you and you're sitting right next to me."

Toby stood up, "Let me have a kook around to see where we are.

"What," Rain sounded surprised, "It's pitch black in here, how are you going to look around?"

Toby tried to laugh a little, "I'll let my walking stick be my eyes. Now you stay here and don't move so I don't lose you." Toby felt the wall with his staff, He and Rain were in a corner. There was a larger passage leading away from them into the dark unknown, and the narrower one leading back the way he had come that went about twelve feet to the incline. If trapped in the smaller passageway it would be impossible to get past the stone nightmare created by Dr. Zodd.

He made his way back to Rain, "Hi, did you miss me," he was trying to lighten her spirits.

"No, of course not, I could smell you all the time. How long since you've showered anyway?"

"Oh, its been a day or two or maybe even four," Toby was glad she was in better spirits, he continued, "Are you feeling better now?"

"Yeah, but I still don't know how we'll get out of here with our skins on. Did you get any bright ideas with your walking stick's Eyes?"

Toby reached down and opened the parcel of cookies the old woman had made for him, "Yeah, there might be a way, here, have a cookie, I'll bet your starving.

Rain took a bite, "Wow, these are really good, where did you get them?"

"An old woman named Ashpit Ashley made them for me, she also gave me this beautiful cape I'm wearing that you can't see. I have more cookies if you want one."

Rain shook her head even though Toby couldn't see her, 'No, one is plenty, they are pretty big, I could use a drink though, do you happen to have any water with you?"

Toby handed her the flask the old hermit had given him, "Here, drink all you want, I have plenty."

She took a couple of drinks, "Are you sure, this doesn't feel like very much water for the two of us, if we manage to get out of here!" She paused for a moment, "Now you said you thought there might be a way, would you like to tell me how?"

Suddenly there was a lot of noise, like rocks falling on the stone floor somewhere in the dark passageway, not far from where they were standing. Toby gently pushed Rain back to the corner where she had been tied. He stood beside her with his back against the wall and his shoulder against the side wall leading from the corner. He pulled her close to him.

"I don't have time to explain what's going on so you need to trust me. Now we need to start making lots of noise."

"What" Rain said loudly, "What are we going to do, simply try to scare it away? This thing sees in the dark and a couple of noisy kids won't scare it a bit!"

"Yeah, that's what I'm counting on" Toby said loudly. Then he started shouting as loud as he could, "Shoo!, go away!, scat!, come and get us!" Rain gasped,

"What's the matter with you." "Here we stand with our backs to a stone wall, no place to go, and you're trying to get that thing to charge us."

Toby squeezed her hand, "Just trust me," then he let out a couple of loud whistles.

The sound of the minotaur's stone hoofs striking the rock floor of the maze sounded like thunder on a dark night. The sounds echoed up and down the many corridors of the maze making it impossible to know exactly where they were coming from. Then came a loud "MOOEEEEeee that made shivers go up and down Toby's back. Rain stood rigid shaking with fear. Toby whistled again and the hoof beats became much quicker and were getting closer to where they were standing. Toby looked into the darkness and could see sparks flying from the stone hoofs of the monster as they struck the solid rock floor of the maze. Again it let out a loud "MOOOEEEeee. It was coming down the passageway at full speed, It's red glaring eyes focused on its prey just ahead. Toby stuck his hand in his satchel of phosphorus dust and just before the raging monster was on top of them he threw a large handful of it into the air, and at the same time gave Rain a hard shove to the side and followed, falling on top of her.

There was a very bright flash followed by a loud crash then several smaller crashing sounds, like large rocks falling on the floor of the maze. The phosphorus dust lit up the corridor enough to see the huge stone statue of the minotaur lying motionless on the floor, it's huge head shattered into several pieces scattered all around. Its neck was broken off from the body and its arms were all busted with the pieces scattered everywhere.

Rain slowly sat up and gasped at the pile of rocks laying around them on the floor.

"What happened?"

Toby smiled a little, "Master Diggers gave me this satchel of phosphorus dust to mark a trail at night." "He also told me that if I threw a handful of the stuff into the air it would make a very bright flash. So I figured that if the minotaur could see in the dark, then a bright flash would probably blind it for a couple of seconds. All we had to do was step out of the way at the right time and let it crash into the wall, just like playing dodge ball at school. I was hoping it would knock itself out, but it totally destroyed itself."

Rain shrugged, "Dodge ball, what's that?"

Toby laughed, "I'll have to show you how to play it sometime, right now we need to find our way out of here."

Chapter 13

A Light At The End Of The Tunnel

Toby grabbed his walking stick and stood up, then reached down and took Rains arm to help her up.

"Wow, you're ice cold."

"Yeah," Rain paused, her teeth chattering, "I feel like I'm freezing. I've been stuck in this frigid chamber for three days now and whoever it was that tied me here couldn't have cared less if I froze."

Toby took off his cape, "Here, put this on, it's nice and warm."

Rain reached over, groping in the dark, took the cape and put it around her shoulders. "Oh, thank you, it feels great, but I don't want you to get cold."

Toby grabbed her arm again, "Oh I'll be fine, I'm wearing two shirts, jeans and heavy socks. Now, lets start trying to find our way out of this black nightmare. Stay close so we don't get separated,"

Toby started feeling the way with his wooden staff. He stopped every fifteen or twenty steps and dropped a pinch of phosphorus dust.

"What's that for Rain asked?"

"It's to mark our way so we can look back and see where we have been. If we run into a dead end we can go back and look for a side passage going a different direction. This way we won't just be going around in circles and getting nowhere."

"Oh, okay," Rain sounded confused.

"Clunk," Toby's staff hit a stone wall. He dropped two pinches of dust. "Now we need to go back and find a side passage, this one ends right here.

"Why didn't we find one before we got to this dead end?"

Toby thought for a moment, "We need to take each passageway as far as it goes, it could be the one that takes us out of here, if it ends like this one, then we go back and try a different one, since I'm marking where we have been we won't be going back the same way we've come. Besides that, I have been checking the wall on my left side and if there had been an opening I would have marked it with three pinches of dust. Since there wasn't, we need to check the wall on the other side till we find another passage. This way takes a while but it the only way to find our way out of here in the dark."

"O-K," I was just asking," Rain chuckled under her breath.

Toby was tapping his staff on the wall while they were talking, "Here it is," Toby dropped three pinches of dust to mark the new opening. Rain was quiet. "Are you still with me?"

"Yes, I'm right behind you, with all that tapping with your stick and all your chitter-chatter there's no way I could get lost."

Toby laughed a little, he knew she was joking. He was glad she was in better spirits and thought he would keep her talking. "O-K," "Since you're bored with my talking, you talk a little, What were you doing in here?"

"Welllllll, in case you've lost your memory, I was tied up waiting to be dinner for some hideous stone monster that bashed its head into a hundred pieces against a stone wall,' Remember."

"That's not quite what I meant, How did you get taken to this temple of Dr. Zodds' in the first place?"

"Well" Rain paused, "I was out in the prairie behind the cemetery picking some wild prairie violets to put on my mothers grave. They were always her favorite flowers and will only grow in the wild. I noticed a huge bird or something circling high overhead but didn't pay any attention to it. Suddenly, without any warning it swooped down and grabbed me by the shoulders with some huge claws and carried me away. It kept going higher and higher and made funny squawking noises. I was afraid it was going to drop me or eat me but it didn't. Instead, it put me down by some old women picking leaves from a tree and putting them in a basket, then flew off to some high rocks."

"When the women saw me, three of them came over, grabbed me, and put a hood over my head. I couldn't see anything but I could hear them talking about me. One of them said, "She'll do really fine, Dr. Zodd was right, she looks as pure as spring water and will make a wonderful meal for the minotaur. They tied my hands together, then one led me by the rope and another followed behind, giving me a little shove every so often. I couldn't see where they were taking me. Finally one of them said, "Well, here we are and tied my hands to that iron ring and left. I managed to shake the hood off my head but all I could see was darkness."

Toby stopped for a moment, 'Do you see what I see." Rain walked up beside him and looked. Up ahead they could see the dim glow of light coming from a side passage and reflecting on the stone wall. "We should soon be out of this black nightmare and back to the outside world of reality.

Chapter 14

I Am Gort

They got to the passageway where the rays of light were coming from and stopped. Only a few hundred feet ahead of them was the opening leading from this black passageway of horrors to the beautiful outside world with sunlight and fresh air. Rain let out a sigh, walked up to Toby and gave him a long hard hug, stepped back and looked him in the eyes,

"Do you realize that if you had been thirty minutes later I wouldn't be standing here by you."

Toby looked at her and smiled, it was a weak smile but still a smile. He still had to get them past the giant guard outside and he wasn't sure just how. He took rains hand, "lets go, but we need to be very quiet. Maybe we can sneak past the giant guard that Dr. Zodd has posted outside. He is not supposed to let anyone come out of the maze."

When they got near the opening, Toby whispered, "Maybe if we're lucky he'll still be sleeping and won't see or hear us. It's still pretty early in the morning.

"Rain nodded, then in a very soft voice, "I can't believe it took almost all night to find our way out of this place," "can you?"

Toby didn't answer, he took Rain by the hand again, held his staff high off the floor so it wouldn't bump anything and started towards the dim opening to the outside world.

They stepped out into the light of early dawn and looked around. There was a pathway leading from the opening with high rock walls on both sides. They started slowly and carefully down it, trying not to make any noise that might alert someone of their presence, and watching closely for any sign of the giant guard. They came to a wider

56

spot in the path where there were the remains of a fire still smoldering on one side and a flat stone on the other side with some food scraps all over it. Rain pointed to them and whispered in Toby's ear.

"Whoever this guy is, he certainly is a slob."

Toby nodded, "Come on, lets keep moving." They took a few more steps when, "CRACK" a huge wooden shaft cane crashing down across the pathway just ahead of them. Toby jumped back, pulling Rain with him. Stepping out from between two big rocks was a huge man.

"WHO GOES THERE?" he growled.

Toby looked up at the man and blinked, he was at least eight or nine feet tall, had a bald head and hair all over his face. His clothes were made from tattered animal skins and he had arms like tree trunks. Rain stepped in front of Toby.

"I'll handle this" she said in a calm voice. "I am the Lady Rainette from Duppland, and this gentleman behind me is Master Toby from the far away land of Brighton. He is my escort and champion. We are returning to Duppland from a mission for the Governess. Please raise your staff so we may pass."

The giant spoke a little louder, "JUST WHAT KIND OF MISSION ARE YOU RETURNING FROM?"

Rain looked up bravely at the huge man, "Master Toby was sent to rescue me from some sort of stone monster back there in the maze and return me home safely."

"WELL LITTLE GIRL," the giant roared, "I don't know how you got past the stone creature back there but I have strict orders from Dr. Zodd not to let anyone coming out of that maze to go pass this point. You may have been able to sneak past that monster, but you can't sneak past me."

"Ha" Rain pointed behind her, "we didn't have to sneak past that pile of rocks, it's laying back there with its head bashed into a million pieces. Now, kindly step aside and let us pass peacefully so I don't have to have my champion trounce you."

Toby gulped, "What did you say?" The giant looked at Toby,

"You're going to have that runt trounce me?"

Rain looked straight up into the giants huge face, "Yes, you may be very big and ugly but I doubt that you are very tough, so please step aside so we don't have to step over you."

Toby pulled on Rains arm, "What are you trying to do, get me killed?"

Rain whispered, "I'm trying to bluff him."

Toby gulped, "Well guess what, it's not working at all."

The giant picked up his staff and raised both arms high in the air, "Since I am the bigger, stronger and undoubtedly the best warrior, I shall give you the opportunity to strike the first blow. Come forward now and show the lady just what kind of champion you really are." Toby slowly stepped forward and looked up at the giants massive shoulders, then down his muscular body to his feet. The giant was wearing open toed sandals. His big toe looked almost as big as Toby's fist. The giant was getting inpatient, "Come on, lets get with it, what are you waiting for, help from the girl?"

Toby slowly raised his walking stick as high as he could, then with both hands slammed it down as hard as he could right on the giants big toe.

"YEHOOoow" the giant bellowed, then dropped his staff and bent down to grab his toe. "You little runt, I'm going to," but before he could finish Toby had raised his staff again and brought it crashing down on the giants other big toe. "YEHOOoow," the huge man roared and bent down to grab his other big toe with his other hand. The giants head was now at a perfect height, Toby raised his staff high over his head an it came crashing down on the back of the giants head so hard it nearly flew from Toby's hands. The giants eyes rolled back and closed and he toppled over to one side.

Rain grabbed Toby by the arm, "Come on," "We don't need to step over him, we can simply walk around him."

Toby nodded, "Yeah, and we need to hurry before he wakes up, he's going to be really, really mad when he does."

Rain smiled, "So will Dr. Zodd."

Toby looked at his walking stick and thought, "Guess there's still a little magic left in you," he didn't want to tell Rain that his staff had been given some magical powers by Zelda and the others, he wanted her to think he had toppled the giant all on his own.

Chapter 15

More

They came to the end of the stone walls along the path and it opened up into a vast wasteland of nothing but rocks, scrubby looking trees and ugly, half dead bushes. Toby turned to the left on a trail that went between a roll of shoddy, tall houses made from dirt bricks. Rain grabbed Toby's arm.

"Do you know where we are going? This looks like the village of the giants!"

"Well, yeah, kind of, I was told to head south "IF" we got out of the maze and past good old Gort back there. According to your sun, this way is south, besides that, it's still early in the morning and hopefully, most of those oversized bullies will still be sleeping."

As they walked quietly between the rows of houses that kind of resembled Indian Pueblo's Toby had seen pictures of in school, he noticed a few giants were already awake. When they saw him and Rain bravely walking down the middle of the road they all kind of ducked back behind trees or into doorways and watched quietly as the two young ventures passed. One very large woman ran out of a hut, grabbed up her two young kids that were playing out front and scampered back into the house.

Rain looked at Toby, "Looks like news travels fast out here. Everyone seems to know you defeated their champion, and it only took three blows."

Toby nodded, "That's all well and good but lets hustle. I don't feel like facing another one of these guys, they scare the pants off me."

Rain looked down and shook her head, "Nooo, I don't think so, You're still wearing yours." They both giggled a little and started walking faster.

They walked out of the village of mud huts and smoke and into the vast openness of the north country. The dirt and rock road between the rows of houses became a narrow pathway, winding its way around stones and scrubby bushes that seemed to be trying to block anyone from passing.

Rain tugged on Toby's arm, "Hey, I'm getting hungry, do we have anything to eat?"

He led Rain over to some flat rocks, sat down and opened the pouch that the cooks back in Duppland had fixed for him. "I still have some biscuits, some dried meat that doesn't taste too bad, and some dried fruit. There is also two cookies left."

Rain gave Toby's arm a little squeeze and smiled, "Since we have such a variety to choose from, lets eat the cookies first. We can save the rest for later when we're really desperate."

Toby nodded, "Good choice," he carefully unwrapped the last two cookies and handed one to Rain.

They finished their cookies, both took a couple of drinks of water, and stood up. Rain looked at Toby with a puzzled look on her face, "You say we're going south and you can tell this by the sun. How will you know which way is south when the sun is right over our heads? I've heard of people being lost and going in circles for days."

Toby pointed to some columns of smoke on the horizon. "Those should be the Lava Pits of Morax. Once we pass those we will turn south-west till we reach the forest of Haggardly, then we'll be almost home."

Rain pointed to Toby's flask, "Will we have enough water to get us that far, I know we've both drank quite a bit but it still seemed full. When did you stop and fill it?"

Toby smiled, "I'm sure we'll be all right, it holds more water than you think. He picked up his walking stick, smiled at Rain and said kind of musically, "Are we ready to go "Me Lady?"

Rain smiled, "Yes "Me Lord" "yonder adventure awaits."

Toby shook his head, "Where did you learn this cheesy talk, sounds like something from Robin Hood back in the 1400s. He was a famous outlaw who lived in a forest in England and was quite a ladies man."

Rain laughed, "Actually it was from a play written by someone named Shakespear." "We've been studying his works in school. We have some of the same books in our literature class as you do. Remember, most of our ancestors came from your land many years ago."

Toby pointed behind them, "Well you should have studied harder, it sure didn't fool that giant back there one little bit."

Rain, trying to sound indignant, "OH" "He was just too dumb to appreciate good literature, now lets get going."

Toby nodded, "Yeah, lets go."

They started walking towards the plumes of smoke from the lava pits, carefully stepping around the sharp rocks and funny looking cactus with long pointed thorns.

Rain pointed, "Oh look" we must be getting close, I can smell smoke and I see a column of it not far ahead."

Toby nodded, "Yeah," "I see it too, but I don't think its coming from the lava pits. When we get to the top of this hill we should be able to tell where its coming from."

They stopped at the top of the hill and looked around. A little ways down the path was a dome shaped mud and sod hut with a column of smoke coming from a hole in the center of its top. There were some trees growing around it and some colorful rocks lining a pathway from the trail to the entrance. Toby looked at the smoke coming from the lava pits, they were just a little ways past the hut and much closer than Toby had expected.

"We should be able to make the lava pits in a couple of hours. Maybe when we reach them we can find a safe place to stop and rest. I know you must be really tired, I sure am, we've been going without sleep for almost two days now."

Rain looked at Toby, "I could lay down right in the middle of this rocky trail and sleep like a baby except for one thing."

Toby laughed, "Oh yeah, what's that?"

'Well, I think we're going to have a visitor very soon," she pointed to a very tall man walking towards them carrying a long pole and had some furry looking animals tied to his side. Rain raised her arm and waved, "Look, he's waving to us."

Toby gasped, "I hope he's waving to be friendly, and not just to trounce us." The giant walked up to the two tired, scared travelers. He was very tall, even taller than Gort. He smiled, held out his hand and in a sort of friendly voice said,

"Hello, my name is More, and what is yours?"

Toby stammered, "This is Rain from Duppland and I am Toby from a land known as Brighton." He looked at the giants extended hand and held his out. The giant took Toby's hand between his thumb and forefinger and gently shook it a few times, then he nodded to Rain, "I am very pleased to meet you, "ma'am"

Toby let out a sigh of relief, his hand wasn't crushed and the huge man seemed to be friendly. The giant pointed to the domed hut, "That's where I live with my mate. We seldom get any travelers along this way, where are you two headed?"

Rain stood up, "Back to Duppland, we hope to be there by tomorrow evening."

The giant looked towards the lava pits, "Well, I've never been there, but I here it's not far from the lava pits. Are you two hungry?"

Toby shook his head, "Naugh, we had something to eat on the trail a little ways back."

Rain stepped forward, "What do you mean not hungry, We're starving. All we've had to eat for two days is a couple of cookies and a few drinks of water."

The giant smiled, "Why don't you come into my shelter and I'll have my mate fix us something to eat, I'm quite hungry also."

Chapter 16

This Is Nickle

Rain and Toby followed More through a very high door that led into the hut, then down a short hallway that opened into a very large circular room. There was another door on the far side that probably went outside to the rear of the hut. In the center of the room was a raised fire pit with a large flat stone that covered about half of a slow burning fire that was probably used to cook on. On one side of the fire pit was a high, flat stone that appeared to be used as a table and there were four very high wooden stools arranged neatly behind it. More pointed to the stools,

"Please have a seat, I will tell Nickle, she's my mate, that we will be having two guests for dinner tonight. She will be thrilled, we don't very often have guests out here in this remote area." Rain and Toby climbed up on the high wooden stools as gracefully as they could, trying not to look too helpless. The giant looked at them, smiled and nodded, then disappeared out the back entrance.

Toby whispered to Rain, "I don't like this, not one bit, he's being too nice to us. I hope when he said he would like to have us for dinner, he didn't mean to eat."

Rain put her finger to her lips, "Shesssss, Toby, you are a mess, quit thinking that everyone here is out to get us. I'm sure these are two very nice people."

The giant came back into the room followed by a nice looking, very tall lady. She was carrying a basket woven from brown colored twigs and filled with different kinds of fruits and vegetables. The giant proudly pointed to her with his open hand and introduced her,

"This is my mate "Nickle." She smiled and nodded at her two guests.

Rain spoke up, "My name is Rain and I come from Duppland, this young man with me is Toby, and he comes from a far away country called Brighton. It truly is a pleasure to meat you and More."

The lady smiled and pointed to More, "When he said we were having guests for dinner I collected some fresh produce from our garden while More cleaned five rabbits for our dinner. I hope you find them satisfactory to you're taste."

Rain grinned, "Oh I like rabbit very much, and I am sure Toby is very happy knowing that rabbit is what's on the menu," "Right Toby?"

Toby looked down sheepishly and grunted, "Uh Uh."

Nickle smiled, "Great, the cooking surface is already hot so everything should ready to eat shortly." She sat the basket on the stone table and smiled, "Aren't you the young man who laid Gort out cold with only three blows?"

Toby gulped, "Yes ma'am."

She shook her head, "That's amazing, no one has ever even been able to even knock him off his feet before. Everyone in the village is talking about the "Boy Wonder." They all seem to think you have super powers or something."

Rain chimed in, "Naugh, he doesn't have super powers, he was just showing off trying to impress me."

Nickle smiled again, "Well I must say he certainly impressed a lot of folks around here."

Toby looked up, "Can I ask a question?"

More and Nickle looked at each other, Nickle nodded, "Yes, you certainly may, what is it you want to know?"

Toby thought for a second, "How did everyone find out so fast that we crossed paths with Gort?"

More laughed, "I guess you wouldn't know this but all giants are telepathic, we are all born with that ability. It is really handy out here in this barren country and is our only way of communicating with someone at a distance. I still have a few friends in the village that I stay in touch with even though I left it when Dr. Zodd turned into such an evil tyrant. He tried to make slaves out of us male giants to serve in his army under the command of a Major Zorn who is said to be Dr. Zodd's half brother. There are twelve or thirteen of us living out here on this wasteland but we have learned to make the best of it. I will let the others know that you will be passing through so you won't have any problems."

While they were talking the tall lady had cut all five rabbits in halves, rubbed some seasoning on them and laid them side by side on the flat cooking stone over the open fire. She also laid several different looking vegetables on the cooking stone above where the rabbits were. Everything was starting to cook and smelled really good. Nickle flipped the rabbits over so they could finish cooking, "Everything should be done shortly, hope you two are hungry, I've cooked a lot of food."

Toby sniffed, "Wow, it really smells great, it's been days since we've had a hot meal."

More stood up and pointed to the rear door, "Why don't you two step out back where you can wash up a little. There is a natural spring that runs into a large stone bowl which makes for a great wash basin. The water is warm and it's always fresh and clean."

When Toby and Rain came back into the hogan Nickle had four plates piled high with food ready to serve. She motioned for her guests to be seated and handed them each a plate, handed one to More, then sat down beside Rain with hers. The food was delicious, there was meat, vegetables, and fresh sweet berries with crushed nuts sprinkled over the top. Nickle looked at Rain,

"What kind of name is Rain?, I think it is very pretty."

Rain swallowed her last bite of berries, "I'm not really sure, my grandfather says my mother named me Rain because that's what it was doing when I was born. I think Nickle is a pretty and very interesting name for a lady, it sounds kind of mysterious and cordial, then she looked over at More, "What kind of name is More? I don't believe I've ever heard it before."

Nickle laughed, "Well when he was born his father looked at him and couldn't get over how big he was. "He said "WOW" there's MORE to this kid than any kid I've ever seen before, and the name More stuck with him ever since. And, it still fits him, there's still more to him than anyone else around." They all looked at him and laughed.

Rain jumped up and carried their plates over to the large table behind the fire that was now burning very low and dimly lighting the large room.

Toby stood up, stretched and yawned, "I guess we should get going, we need to find somewhere near the lava pits where we can rest till morning."

Nickle jumped up, she seemed to be the boss over the house and More, "You certainly will not, it's almost dark outside and it's not safe to be on the trail at night, is it More?", she didn't wait for him to answer, "We have sleeping areas all around the dome and there is plenty of space where the two of you can safely rest till morning. Then you can leave and be well past the lava pits by midday."

Rain looked at Toby, "I am really tired, are you sure we wouldn't be a burden?"

"Absolutely not, it's nice to have guests in our home once ever so often," Nickle sounded pleased that they were staying.

"Ouch", Toby felt a sharp pain in his leg.

"Come on," "Wake up," It's morning" Rain was standing over him kicking his leg. "Get up you lazy bum, Nickle has fixed breakfast for us."

Toby sniffed, he could smell eggs and some sort of meat cooking. He staggered to his feet, "Wow, it really smells good. All this sleep really made me hungry."

Rain shook her head and pointed to the rear door, "Go out there and freshen up a bit, we'll all be out there with our plates, I'll bring yours. We're eating in the garden, sounds exciting doesn't it?"

Toby was amazed when he stepped out into the garden. More had stacked stones to form a wall around the back side of the hogan that looked much like a large courtyard. There were fruit trees, bushes with berries on them and different plants growing everywhere. He could hear some clucking sounds like chickens make coming from behind the wall. Right in the middle sat a large stone table with benches around it where everyone was sitting.

"Come on," Rain called, "Your food will get cold."

Toby pushed his plate back, "Thank you, That was very good."

More nodded, "My Nickle is a great cook, I don't know what I would have done if she hadn't come with me when I left Dr. Zodd's compound, I would feel lost without her.

Toby looked up at More, "Is this the same Dr. Zodd who supposedly came to this land over four hundred years ago?"

More nodded, "Yes, when he and the rest of his coven appeared out of nowhere, everyone believed they were gods sent here to show us a better way to live, at least, that's what Dr, Zodd wanted all of us to believe. He formed a work crew and made them work day and night to build his secret temple with that horrid maze you two were trapped in. Then he made two of our best sculpturers create that hideous looking stone monster that he somehow gave life to, using a power he calls mind over matter that he somehow developed. It seems that as his powers got greater he would use them to totally control everyone in the compound. It is said that he discovered a very special tree that could slow down the ageing process by drinking tea made from its leaves. I guess that is why he is still alive today. The longer he lives, the more wicked and evil he gets, and the greater his powers become. No one dares to challenge him or dis-obey his orders."

More took a sip from a cup he was holding, "Dr. Zodd. is one to be feared, no one knows where he stays, he just appears every few days to inspect the compound. He has placed Major Zorn in charge of overseeing the community and also to develop an army of loyal giants. So far he's not been very successful finding volunteers for the army and has threatened to use other means if necessary. Who knows what that might be? Well, that's all I can tell you about the evil Dr., he doesn't bother us out here and we don't go looking for him."

Toby and Rain stood up, Rain smiled, "Thank you very much for your hospitality. I believe Toby and I need to be on our way. We have a long way to go today. You have both been very kind."

Nickle stood up, "Let me fix you a bag of fruit and nuts to take with you, they'll give you energy and something to snack on while walking."

Chapter 17

The Lava Pits Mercer

Toby and Rasin looked back at their two new friends who were standing in the doorway of their hut, smiling and waving good-by. The two young ventures smiled and waved back, then focused their attention to the trail leading toward the lava pits.

Rain nudged Toby, "See, aren't you glad we stopped? I told you that everyone we meet wouldn't be out to get us."

Toby smiled, "Well since they all communicate telepathically, and you can do the same, I suspect that you knew more about their intentions than I did."

She grinned, "Could be, could be."

The path leading to the lava pits was getting narrower and Rain had to follow behind Toby to keep from brushing up against the caucus and thorny bushes along the sides of the trail.

Toby turned and looked back at Rain, "We're almost to the first lava pit, it's just a little ways ahead. We need to be sure and watch for lava snakes, they are treacherous."

Rain nodded, and tugged on Toby's arm, "Can I get a drink?, it's really getting hot."

Toby stopped and shook the water flask, it felt full, he removed the cap and handed it to Rain. She took a big drink, then a smaller sip and handed it back.

"Boy, that water is cool and really taste good, did you fill it at the giants hut?"

Toby took a big drink and replaced the top, "It is nice and cool" he said, avoiding her question, he liked for her to think he was taking care of things.

Toby looked up at the sun, "Guess we better get going again before the sun gets too high, it will really get hot out here around noon. He took a step forward then jumped back, bumping into Rain, almost knocking her down.

"What's the matter? Are you okay?"

Toby nodded, "Yeah," "I'm fine," "but there's a lava snake just ahead and I almost stepped on it."

Rain thought for a moment, "Pour some water on its head from that amazing water flask you have, that should stop it."

Toby reached out in front of him with the opened flask and carefully poured some water directly on the glowing snakes head. The long body of the snake started whipping from side to side but it didn't go anywhere. The cool water hissed and turned into steam and at the same time turned the snakes head to solid stone rendering it helpless. Toby replaced the cap on the flask that was still full of water and looked back at Rain, "You're right, that worked great." She nodded and smiled.

Toby started out again, "Stay close behind me and watch both sides of the path for those things, I'll be watching ahead. They walked slowly and cautiously down the trail past two of the thirteen smoking lava pits, then the path split and went two different directions. One went through the middle of the pits and the other seemed to go around all of them.

Toby stopped and looked back, "Why do you suppose the trail splits here? One way looks easy, the other looks dangerous and hard."

Rain thought for a moment, "The easy way is probably a trap of some sort, we should take the hard way, it's probably safer."

Toby shrugged, "Yeah, you're probably right again, we'll do it the hard way."

They started down the trail leading through the sizzling lava pits. They were like huge craters in the ground with the centers bubbling and spewing out red hot ashes and flaming cinders high into the air, which were falling to the ground around them like glowing rain drops.

"Ouch!, Ouch!, Toby, help me!"

Toby looked back at Rain, Her shirt sleeve was on fire. He grabbed his flask of water and quickly doused the flames. Then he took the cape she had tucked under her arm and thoroughly wet it.

"Here, hold this end over your head and I'll hold the other end over mine, it will keep the sparks and hot ashes off of us."

She nodded, her eyes were full of tears, "Are we going to be alright, I'm really scared."

Toby tried to sound brave and sure of himself, "Of course we will, we just need to go slow and watch for the snakes, The cape will keep us from getting burned and we have plenty of water." He didn't want her to know that this was turning into the worst day of his life and it was still only morning. They were out in the middle of thirteen small volcanoes all trying to erupt around them, and if they made it out they still had to cross several miles of waste land and who knows what else before they reached the forest of Haggardly and Duppland.

Slowly the two young travelers wove their way between the smoldering infernals, only stopping from time to time to pour some water on a thin line of lava that resembled a snake with its mouth opened. Finally, after what seemed like hours they passed the last lava pit and out of the shower of sparks and cinders and lowered the cape from over their heads. Rain shook her arms,

"Whew, I'm glad that's over, my arms got really tired holding that cape over our heads."

Toby nodded, "Yeah, mine too."

The wide open, endless looking wasteland ahead was a welcome sight even though they had no idea what pearls they could run into. Toby pointed, "Look up ahead, there's a large shade tree with some rocks around it. We can sit for a few minutes, enjoy the shade and have a few berries and nuts Nickle gave us."

After a few minutes they reached the tree and selected a rock that was large enough for both to sit on. The berries and nuts tasted really good. They sat quietly enjoying the trail mix Nickle had given them, occasionally pausing to brush aside a small bee that was trying to get in on the feast.

Rain rubbed her stomach, "I think I've eaten plenty, is there enough water for us each to have a small drink?"

Toby smiled and handed her the flask. She shook it and slowly removed the top, "I don't believe this, it's still full. When did you stop to fill it? There was no water back there!"

Toby just smiled and looked around. "Do you have any idea which way it is to Duppland from here? I know its southwest but the sun is high in the sky and I have no idea which way is south, do you?"

Rain moaned, "Oh brother," I guess you didn't even think about bringing a compass, did you?"

Toby looked around, "A compass, what's that?"

"That's not a bit funny" she sneered.

Chapter 18

The Waste Lands Of Azzure

Toby stood up, looked around, walked over to a long straight twig that had fallen from the tree and picked it up.

"This should work fine as a compass."

Rain frowned, "You've got to be kidding."

"Nope" Toby replied as he pulled the gold handled pocket knife from his pocket and started to sharpen one end of the stick, "I'm sure it can show us which way is west. He finished sharpening the stick, put the knife back in his pocket then walked out of the shade and into the bright sunlight. He picked up a good sized rock and gently tapped the stick into the ground so that it pointed up towards the sun, backed away a couple of steps to admire his work, "There, that should work fine."

He walked over to the flat rock and sat down beside Rain, "There, now we can rest for a while."

Rain jumped up with her hands on her hips, "I think you've finally lost it, here we are out here in the middle of nowhere, probably lost, and you stick a old dead tree limb in the ground and say everything's fine, so lets rest awhile! We have very little food, I have no idea how much water, but I do know that we can't survive out here forever. If you have a plan, you need to tell me, O K."

Toby stood up, put his arm around her shoulders, and pulled her to him. "Yes, I have a plan, when I stuck the stick into the ground it was straight up and didn't cast any shadow. Now since the sun sets in the east in your land, as it slowly moves that way it will cast a shadow on the west side of the stick. We won't be able to tell the sun has moved since it will still be high overhead, but the stick is long enough so that the shadow cast from the suns movement will be on the west side of the stick. Once we have that we can draw a line in the dirt straight down from it on the left side and that will point to the south." "Then if we draw a line from the stick right between the two, that way will be south-west." "Then all we need to do is find a reference point south-west on the horizon and walk towards it. We should be able to get started in about thirty minutes." Rain slowly shook her head as Toby sat back down on the rock and leaned back.

After a short while Toby stood up and stretched, "We should be getting started now, I enjoyed our little rest."

Rain looked around, "Do we know which way we need to be going?, I'd hate to be walking the wrong direction."

Toby pointed to the stick, "See, the shadow, it's pointing towards the west, we need to be going a little to the left from the way it is pointing and that is south-west. See I told you we weren't lost."

"Well, we're not there yet either so grab your little stick and your big stick and lets go." Toby wasn't sure if she was trying to be sarcastic or funny, he did know that the last four or five days had been very trying on her so he just kept quiet.

Toby picked up his staff, snatched the pointed stick from the ground and headed off across the endless wasteland of Azzure in the direction he figured was south-west. He looked across the horizon for some sort of reference point to guide them so they wouldn't veer off in the wrong direction, but all he could see was flat wasteland. Rain followed behind quietly, stopping once in a while to pick up a rock or something, look at it, then toss it aside. Toby wondered if he had done something to make her mad. He figured it would be best not to ask her, she would tell him when she was ready.

Toby could look back behind them and still see the plumes of smoke coming from the lava pits. Once they were out of sight, with no trail to follow and no reference point to guide them, it would be easy to start going in the wrong direction. Toby stopped, took the top from the flask of water and handed it to Rain.

"Thank you" she said softly, took a long drink, handed it back to Toby and gave him a smile, "Thanks, that was good." Toby nodded, took a long drink, replaced the top and looked in the direction they were going. Off in the distance he could see a small rock formation. It was in line with the lava pits and gave him the reference point he was looking for. He pointed to the pile of rocks,

"we will stop for a short breather when we reach those rocks and have a bite to eat."

Rain smiled, "I'm for that, all this walking really gives me an appetite."

When they finally reached the rock formation they shared some of the berries and nuts that Nickle had packed for them, then washed down sone dry biscuits and meat jerky with water from the flask. Toby looked at the rocks. There were four large rocks all piled against each other. On top of the biggest one was another very large rock that looked to be balanced on it witch reminded him of an hourglass. He looked at Rain,

"You stay here, I'm going to climb up on top of these rocks to see if I can spot another reference point to guide us when we start out again." Rain nodded and leaned against one of the rocks. Toby leaned his staff against the rock next to her and started climbing up the formation. He got to the top of the biggest rock when he heard Rain gasp,

"Toby, Toby,"

Toby looked down, Rain was backed up flat against one of the giant rocks. Just in front of her was a huge reptile, its mouth opened wide and it made a horrible "Hisssaaah" sound. Toby couldn't believe his eyes, it looked like a Komono Dragon he had seen on T V only much larger. It had rows of yellowish-brown teeth and long strings of drool hanging down from its lower jaw. He remembered them saying on T V that if it didn't eat you, you would still probably die from its bite because of all of the germs and deadly bacteria in its mouth.

Toby looked at Rain, his walking stick was still leaning against the rock right next to her. "Rain" Toby said calmly, "Slowly raise my walking stick so I can reach it, then be very quiet and don't move, I'll try to get its attention away from you with my staff."

Rain nodded. and whispered, "Hurry, I'm really scared" and slowly raised the staff up to him.

Toby took the long pole, raised it high over his head and slammed it down on the dragons rear end. The dragon spun around looking up at its new victim. Toby thought, "Now I've got you right where I want you, just don't move." He started whistling hoping to keep the dragons attention while he went to work on the balanced rock. He placed his staff under the backside and pried up as hard as he could. The huge rock tottered a couple of times then rolled off the edge of the bigger rock, making a funny squishing sound when it hit the ground. Toby looked down. The rock had found its mark, landing right in the middle of the dragons back.

Toby slid down the rock. Rain was still shaking with fear and looking at the pile of green and grey scales that was crushed under the fallen rock. She looked at Toby, wrapped her arms around him and gave him a long hug. Toby looked into her eyes and smiled,

"That was kind of scary, wasn't it?"

Rain pushed him away, "What do you mean "Kind Of? You weren't the one on the ground he was drooling over.

Toby nodded, "Yeah, but you didn't have anything to worry about, it probably thought you were too skinny and boney to make a good meal." She looked at him and gave him a weak smile.

Chapter 19

Help From Afar

The two companions started out again, heading in the direction they hoped was south-west. The way was rocky and the going was slow. After about a hour Toby looked back at Rain. She had stopped and was about thirty or forty yards behind him. He knew she had to be getting tired because he was. The last few days had been harder than he had ever imagined. He was starting to have doubts weather or not they would make it back to Duppland, but he knew they needed to keep going. He had heard stories about pioneers and explorers who were trying to get somewhere that was difficult but never made it because they gave up when they only had a little way farther to go.

Toby waved and called to Rain, "Come on, We need to keep going, it's not much farther now." Rain started walking slowly, looking down at the sharp rocks and thorns and trying to avoid them the best she could. When she reached Toby she looked very hot and tired and her feet were a mess. She was only wearing light sandles and her feet and ankles were bruised and bleeding. Toby pulled his pocket knife from his pocket and cut off both sleeves from his shirt. "Here, put these on your feet like stockings, they should give you a little protection from the rocks and stubble we're in. Rain took the sleeves, removed her shoes and slid them over her feet, then slipped her shoes on over them. "Thank you she said while wiping a tear from her eye. Sorry I got behind, but I had some meditating to do, do we have any water left?" Toby nodded, took the top from his flask of water and handed it to her.

"Thank you, I can't believe this thing is always full," then took a long drink and handed it back to him.

Toby took a couple of sips and replaced the top, "Do you feel better now?, maybe if we get going we can reach the forest of haggardly before dark. Toby had no idea if they would ever reach the forest but he wanted to raise Rain's spirits a little.

They had only walked a few steps farther when Rain tapped Toby on the shoulder. She was smiling and pointing out ahead of them to a spot on the horizon. Toby stopped and looked at the spot, it seemed to be moving.

"What do you suppose it is" he asked?

"I hope it's the help I asked Lady Zelda for. I was finally able to communicate with her back there and told her that we might be lost. I described where we were and she said she would send some help. I hope that is it, my feet are killing me."

Toby frowned, "Why didn't you tell me you could communicate with Zelda? "Did you think I didn't need to know. And another thing, Why are you mad at me?"

Rain stood up straight and shook her tiny little fist at Toby, "First of all, I wasn't able to reach Lady Zelda telepathically tell just a little way back, and I just did tell you. Second, I'm not mad at you, I just have a lot on my mind. The last five days have been very hard, and if it weren't for you, my bones would be laying somewhere back in that maze of horror. Now were out here somewhere in no mans land trying to figure out how to get back to Duppland. I know it's all my fault that you're stuck out here with me, but I had to ask for you to save me, no one else in Duppland would have the guts or brains to even try.

Toby patted Rain on the shoulder, "Well don't feel bad, I guess I volunteered, I couldn't let my best friend end up as monster food. And you're right about no one in Duppland having any guts, the two guards Zelda sent with me to help didn't last the first day."

Rain shook her head, "I hope the help Lady Zelda is sending this time will be more reliable."

Toby looked puzzled, "You keep saying she is sending help, What kind of help?" Rain laughed a little.

"Guess we won't know till it gets here. It's been really hard to communicate with her way out here, that's the reason I've been so quiet and ignoring you while we were walking, you can't have gibber-jabber while you're trying to be telepathic with someone. Anyway, the last thing I understood was Help is on the way."

Toby looked out ahead of them, the tiny dot coming towards them had four legs. "What is it?, looks kind of like a small horse."

Rain shrugged, "It's the help she said she would send, that's all I know."

Toby smiled, "Well I guess any help is better than no help at all, especially way out here, and remember this, I would have been really mad if you had asked for someone else to rescue you and not me. Now, lets keep going towards that four legged critter and when we meet it, lets hope it's friendly."

After walking a little ways Toby stopped and pointed, "It's a horse," "It's a white horse with a sword or something sticking out of its head."

Rain burst out laughing, "That's not a horse silly, It's a unicorn."

"A unicorn" Toby gasped, "I thought those things existed only in fairy tails."

The unicorn trotted up to them and nudged the parcel of berries and nuts Toby was carrying. "It must be hungry" Toby said as he opened the parcel and gave the last of its contents to the graceful animal. It quickly finished the berries and nuts then nudged Toby's flask with its nose. Toby handed the flask to Rain, "Here, pour some of this into my hands so it can get a drink." He cupped his hands tightly together and Rain poured water into them till the unicorn had enough to drink. Rain looked into the top of the flask and shook her head, it was still full. She replaced the top and handed it back to Toby,

"You'll have to tell me about this flask sometime, I know it's not you keeping it full." Toby just smiled.

The tall unicorn moved beside Rain and pushed her towards its back with its nose. Toby was shocked, "Look, it wants you to get on.

Rain gently climbed up on its back and slid forward and took a hold of its short mane. Next it looked at Toby and made a funny Neeeeee sound. Rain looked at Toby, "Now its your turn, be careful so you don't poke your heels into its flanks, animals don't like that." Toby stepped up on a rock and gently slid onto the animals back behind Rain.

The graceful animal turned back in the direction it had come and started off in a gentle pace with the two weary travelers on its back. Toby leaned forward and whispered in Rains ear,

"I'm sure glad you were able to get us a ride, I was getting so tired and my feet were hurting so bad that I couldn't have gone much farther."

Rain nodded, "Me too."

Chapter 20

The Evil Gateway

After about four hours of carefully picking its way through the sharp rocks, thorny cactus, and going up and down deep ravines the proud steed and its two weary riders reached a lush green forest. It trotted along the edge till it came to a small opening in the trees and dense shrubs. The powerful animal came to a stop and looked back at its two dozing riders. It gently nudged Toby with its nose to arouse him. He had his arms around Rain's waist and his head resting on her shoulder. Rain was holding onto the animals short mane with both hands to keep from falling off and was slumped forward, probably from the weight of Toby's head.

The unicorn again nudged Toby with its nose, a little harder this time. Toby raised his head, looked around and tapped Rain on her shoulder.

"Hey," "Wake up sleepy head, we're here."

Toby gently slid off the back of the patient beast, then helped Rain as she tried to dismount gracefully, but stumbled a little when her feet hit the ground. They both patted the unicorn on the head and Rain gave it a big hug around the neck. The animal looked at them, gave a little nod then disappeared into the lush greenery of the forest.

Toby pointed to the opening in the trees that led to the narrow pathway that he and the two cowardly guards had emerged from just a few days before.

"Follow me and stay close behind, this is not much of a path and is full of all kinds of thorns, burrs, and old dead branches to trip over. I guess it doesn't get used very often, but it will take us to that larger trail where we followed those shadow people down a couple of years ago."

Rain nodded, "Yeah, I remember them."

Toby used his walking stick to help hold the bushes and tree branches out of the way while they passed. Slowly and carefully they followed the tiny opening through the dense foliage. Rain had to stop occasionally to remove small twigs and burrs that had become tangled in her long blond hair. Toby kept quiet and helped her the best he could, he figured they would soon be on the main trail and the going would be much easier for her.

They continued on the narrow path for about another half hour tell they finally came to the larger trail that would take them back to Dupperville. Toby looked up and sniffed,

"I can smell smoke." He looked at Rain, "Is it possible that's the same burning embers we saw a couple of years ago. He grabbed her hand, "Lets have a look."

Rain thought for a moment, "OK," "But only for a quick glance, that is a very evil place."

The two cautiously walked up the trail and out into the clearing where the fire pit was. The embers were still glowing red with small columns of smoke raising slowly from them and disappeared into the thick canopy of leaves and branches high overhead. Toby looked around,

"I wonder who keeps feeding the fire?, it doesn't look like anyone has been around for a long time."

Rain pulled on Toby's arm, "Come on," "Lets go" "No one ever feeds that fire, I'll tell you more about it while we're walking."

They turned and started down the trail away from the clearing. Toby was having a hard time keeping up with Rain.

"Hey" "Slow down," "You're suppose to tell me about the fire pit, re member."

Rain slowed down a little and looked back, "That burning pit is said to be the gateway to the land of the evil dead and will probably burn forever. As long as it burns the soles of the evil dead can pass back and forth through it but only at night. It is believed that they can cause great harm and sickness to those who try and stop them. I believe one of them had a vengeance for my mother and caused the illness that she died from. Someday I hope I have the powers to avenge her suffering." She paused for a moment, "I guess if they don't get back through the gateway before sunrise the brightness of day will destroy them, at least that's what I've heard. Maybe someday someone will figure out a way to put that fire out and close the gateway."

Toby looked up, "Wouldn't a real hard rain put it out?"

Rain shrugged, "I guess if it got doused with enough water it might go out, but the overhead trees with their thick branches shelter it from the rain like a huge umbrella. Maybe if someone could pour enough water on it, then it might go out, but there's no water around here." They turned and started back down the trail towards Dupperville

They walked in silence for a while till finally they came out of the forest and to the street that would take them to Rains house and her anxiously awaiting grandfather.

Toby looked at Rain smiling, "Well you're almost home." Down the dimly lit street he could see the form of an old man with a walking stick hobbling towards them as fast as his shaking legs would go. Rain ran out to meet him and gave him a big hug. Toby walked up to the happy pair and smiled. Master Boggs took Toby's hand and shook it, and said softly

"It makes me very, very proud to know you and to be able to call you my friend. I knew that if anyone could save Rain and bring her back safely to me it would be you."

Toby looked at the old mans face, There were tears coming from both of his eyes. That made Toby feel great and humble at the same time.

The old man turned towards their home, "Come on, lets go to the house, Rain let me know that you like double cheeseburgers with nothing on them. The town cooks are sending down a couple with plenty of french fries to go with them."

Rain looked up, "What about me, I'm starving too."

"Yeah," "Yeah," "They're sending some grilled cheese sandwiches and fresh fruit for you."

Rain smiled, "Sounds good, come on, lets hurry."

Chapter 21

Shadow Spirits

Even though Toby was exhausted he was having trouble sleeping. The couch he was laying on seemed shorter than it was the last time he slept on it, or perhaps he had grown a bit in the last couple of years. Whatever it was he couldn't get comfortable. He opened his eyes and stared at the open window across the room. There was a faint glow of light shining in from the dim street light that stood across the street. The white, lacy curtains were being tossed leisurely about by a soft summer breeze that managed to find its way through the open window, bringing the fresh smell of newly mowed grass and summer flowers into the room.

Toby laid there thinking about the past few days and the hidden temple where Rain was held. Suddenly Toby was startled by what he thought was a shadow passing in front of the window and then disappear in the darkness of the room. It gave him a very uneasy feeling. He laid motionless peering into the darkness, unable to see anything. He turned his gaze back towards the window thinking that maybe the stories Rain told him about the evil gateway had him imagining things. He was just about to close his eyes again and try to sleep when he saw another shadow pass the window and disappear into the darkness.

Now he was wide awake again, he thought about the two shadow people he saw when he spent the night in the park on his first visit to Duppland. They disappeared into the fire pit of burning embers after he and Rain followed them deep into the forest of Haggardly. It was the same fire pit they had passed on their way back to Dupperville. Could these two shadow people have followed them to Rain's house so they could report back to some evil entity where she stayed? Toby sat up on the couch, the two shadow people must have heard him moving about and floated out the open window, disappearing into the night.

Toby sat there thinking for a moment. He felt he needed to do something to keep the two shadow people from reporting their findings to some evil entity waiting for them on the other side of the gateway.

He stood up, quietly picked up his walking stick and water flask then crept out the front door, closing it silently behind him. He started running down the street towards the park and the forest where the forbidden trail was. He figured the two shadow people were heading there also and he wanted to get there before they did. He was out of breath when he got to the pathway, paused for a moment and looked around. There were no signs of the shadow people so he started down the trail that would take him to the burning fire pit that Rain said was the gateway to the land of the evil dead.

Toby hurried as fast as he could but in the darkness it was hard to see the scrubby bushes, dead branches and other things on the trail which made the going difficult. He tripped a couple of times but he got up and kept going, not stopping to brush himself off or clear the thorns from his hands. Finally he knew he was getting close to the clearing and the fire pit because he could smell the smoke from the burning embers.

He rounded a bend in the trail and could see the clearing where the fire pit would be. He stopped for a minute, then slowly walked up to the burning pile of embers in the middle of the clearing. Fear of the unknown was catching up to him. Back on the trail he was to busy trying to hurry and to keep on his feet to be scared. Now that he was at the clearing he could feel his knees starting to shake and he felt like he was being watched by all kinds of wicked things.

Toby shook off the wave of fear the best he could and starred at the smoldering embers. The fire pit had a circle of rocks around it and there appeared to be two fires burning inside it at the same time. One covered the entire area inside the fire pit, and the second was about half the size of the first and looked to be floating just above it. He shuddered, it did look like an evil place to be but he had a plan that he hoped would work. He remembered what Rain had said about the burning embers and having enough water to put them out. He removed the top from his flask and started pouring water into the smouldering inferno. It sputtered, hissed and made weird noises almost like it was alive. Tongues of flame reached out towards his pant legs and columns of steam and sparks rose up from the embers and went in all different directions, almost like they were being tossed about by a whirlwind.

Slowly the flames and glowing embers started to turn dark and lifeless. Toby hoped the water flask that Mystic Mitizie had put a spell on to never go dry would hold out. The water kept coming and after a while the smoke and glowing embers turned to wet brown ashy mud and rising steam. He continued to pour water on the ashes till they were totally covered with it. Toby stepped back, put the flask to his lips and took a long cool drink. Then he looked into the top and smiled, it was still full. He replaced the stopper, picked up his walking stick and started back down the trail.

He hadn't seen the shadow people since he left Rain's house. He wondered if they had got to the gateway before him and had already passed through to an other dimension, or if they were still floating about somewhere, unaware that their exit from this world had been closed. Either way it didn't matter, If they were still snooping around they wouldn't be able to get back to report anything and would just fade away to nothing at dawn. If they had reached the gateway before him, then they and their evil ways would be sealed where they could do no one any harm.

Toby smiled, he was proud of his feat and decided not to tell anyone about it, it would just be his secret. It was almost daylight when Toby crept through the door. He quietly laid his walking stick and water flask on the floor beside the sofa, stretched out on it the best he could and was immediately asleep.

Chapter 22

The Homecoming

Morning always came to early for Toby, even at ten-thirty. He could feel someone shaking him and a soft voice saying, "Wake up," "common, time to rise and shine. He opened his eyes the best he could and looked around. It was Rain, she was already up and dressed. Toby slowly sat up,

"Boy, I never knew a couch could feel so good." He looked at Rain again and blinked, she was wearing a crisp blue satin dress that matched her blue eyes, silver sandals and her hair was tied back with a silver bow. Toby looked down at his clothes, he was a mess. His shirt was torn several places and had holes burnt in it. One of the legs on his jeans was ripped from the knee down, and his new sneakers were all tattered and filthy.

Rain smiled, "Come on, I'll get you something clean to put on, but first, you need to go into the bathroom and wash up."

She handed Toby a new pair of jeans that looked to be his exact size, a new crisp green shirt, and a new pair of stockings.

"Here, while you're getting into these I'll see to your shoes, boy are they a mess."

Toby looked at the new clothes in amazement.

Rain smiled, "When grandpa knew we were on our way back he gave the village tailors your sizes, and they whipped them out yesterday."

Toby shook his head, "That's really amazing."

Rain smiled, "What's amazing?"

"Telepathic communication, it sure beats a cell phone. You don't have to worry about a dead battery or losing your signal." He shook his head and headed towards the bathroom.

Rain handed Toby his sneakers when he came out.

"Wow" "You really did a great job on my shoes, and these clothes, they fit great, Tell your grandfather thanks. By the way, where is he?"

Rain shrugged a little, "Oh, he's already left, now hurry and get your shoes on so we're not late."

"Late, late for what?"

She smiled, "You'll see."

They stepped out the front door and stopped in their tracks. Waiting for them out in the street was a transport cart. It was decorated with balloons, flags and long streamers. Driving it was one of the elite guards in full uniform, shinny steel helmet, polished saber and a bright green sash tied around his waste. He motioned for Rain and Toby to sit in the back on a raised seat.

They started down the street towards the town square. Toby was confused and nudged Rain,

"What's going on?, Is this some kind of a holiday you have here that I wasn't told about?"

Rain just sat back and smiled. As they got nearer to the town square the streets were lined with cheering spectators all waving to them. Rain smiled, waved back, then kicked Toby on the leg,

"Just don't sit there like a bump on a log, smile a little and wave back. They're all waving to us."

Toby managed to smiled and waved back to the crowd, even though he was embarrassed and his face had turned a bright shade of red. The transport stopped in front of the town square where Lady Laura and

Lady Dana were both waiting to greet them. They each gave Rain a hug and shook Toby's hand, then led them up onto the stage where they were both seated on one side of a long table. Lady Dana and Lady Laura sat across from them leaving one empty chair between them. After a couple of minutes Lady Zelda walked up to the empty chair and sat down. She looked over at Lady Laura and nodded. Lady Laura walked up to the microphone, adjusted the height a little, then held both arms over her head to quiet the crowd.

"Today," she paused, "Today we are very fortunate to have with us a visitor from the other side," "Master Toby," who is indeed a true hero. She paused while the crowd cheered again, then held up an arm to quiet them. "He single handedly rescued Lady Rain who was to be sacrificed to a hideous, living stone creature that lived inside the secret temple of Dr. Zodd. She paused for a moment, "Not only did he rescue her but he totally destroyed the living stone nightmare created by the evil Dr. Now we shall never have to worry about other young women being taken from Duppland to be sacrificed each year, which was Dr. Zodd's intention. His heroic deeds have earned him the respect and highest admiration of Lady Zelda and the quorum of twelve." Lady Zelda stood up and walked over to the microphone.

"Master Toby," "Will you please join me at the microphone?"

Toby sheepishly stood up and walked over to the microphone. Lady Zelda held out her hand,

"On behalf of the quorum of twelve and myself, I would like to shake your hand and thank you for being our special friend." She took Toby's hand and squeezed it very tightly. Toby felt a little funny, his ears started to ring and his eyes got blurry. When she let go of his hand these things slowly went away. She looked at him and smiled.

"Your just reward is coming. She motioned for him to sit down and followed him to the table and to her seat.

Lady Laura stepped back up to the microphone and raised her arms several times trying to quiet the crowd who were cheering "Toby" "Toby" "Toby." Finally the crowd was quiet enough to hear her.

"We have another announcement before we break to the picnic area for lunch. As you all know Lady Zelda has been our governess for over thirty years. Under her rein she has transformed our community from a village of run down huts and shacks to this beautiful township of Duppersville. She formed a departmental type of government that equally distributes the rights and duties of the community to all its adult citizens. She has been a great inspiration and leader for all of us," she paused while the crowd clapped, "After all this, Lady Zelda feels that it is time for her to step down and turn the responsibility of governess over to someone else." The crowd gasped in surprise and disbelief. Lady Laura continued, "The quorum of twelve have been aware of this for sometime and have had the task of selecting another head of state who has the knowledge, leadership and ability to fill this position."

"Now, after many weeks discussing the matter and reviewing all candidates they thought were worthy of this position, they made their decision." "Lady Dana," "It was unanimous that Lady Dana was the best one in Dupperville for this position. She has been Lady Zelda's senior aide for several years and is familiar the responsibilities associated with this undertaking. She will begin her new duties on July first of this year. I will take her position as senior aide and we are appointing a new junior aide. We all know her and love her,"

"Lady Rain," "Lady Rain, will you please come up to the microphone."

Rain stood up and smiled at Toby as he sat there in shock, then stepped over to the microphone. Lady Laura took both of Rain's hands, "Lady Rain, you have heard the decision of the quorum, do you accept this challenge you have been charged with, obeying all the covenants set fourth by the quorum and setting yourself up as an example for all the other young members of our township to respect and follow."

Rain thought for a moment, "Yes, it would be a great honor to accept this charge."

Lady Laura released Rains hands and whispered, "Wave to the crowd." Rain waved with both hands and the crowd cheered wildly, "Rah," "Rah," "Rah," "Rain," "Rain," "Rain." Rain kept waving as she walked back to her seat and sat down next to Toby. He just sat there with a bewildered look on his face, still not sure what had just happened. Lady Zelda reached across the table and nudged Toby's arm.

"I need to see you and Rain in my chambers after you finish your lunch. Take your time and enjoy it, there's no hurry."

Toby nodded, "Yes Mam."

Chapter 23

The Truth

Toby slowly picked at his plate of food. For some reason he wasn't very hungry and only ate about half of his ham and cheese sandwich, a couple of chips and drank about half his glass of orange-lime aide. He pushed his plate back and slowly stood up. One of the servers asked if he had finished? Toby nodded and the server politely removed his half eaten lunch.

He began to look around for Rain. Ever since the announcement of her new position she had been surrounded by young ladies, all excited for her and jabbering all at the same time. He gazed up and down the rows of tables for her shining blue dress and blond hair but she was nowhere to be seen. He stood there wondering about her and her new responsibilities when he felt a light tap on his shoulder,

"Are you ready to go?"

He spun around, Rain was standing there with Lady Laura,

"I was just looking for you at the tables, I didn't know you had finished eating."

Rain smiled, "Laura and I split a sandwich on the other side of that tree where we could talk privately. She will escort us to Lady Zelda's chambers."

Toby nodded, "Yeah, I guess we should go see what she wants to talk to us about."

Rain grabbed Toby's hand and they followed Lady Laura past the rows of picnic tables, still filled with people finishing their lunch and out of the picnic area. They came to a large building with a sign over the door, "GOVERNMENT OFFICES," and in smaller letters, "Restricted

Entry." They followed Laura through the door and down a long hallway. There were doors with names and numbers on both sides. At the end of the hallway was a large double door that opened into a three room suite. There was a large desk in the middle of the main room with two chairs in front and a large, high back padded chair behind it. There was a sign over one of the side rooms that read Library, and there were shelves of books visible through the half opened door.

There was a sing over the door on the other side room that read "Private." Lady Laura pointed to the two chairs.

"please be seated, I shall inform Lady Zelda that you are here."

She walked over to the door marked "Private" and tapped on it. After a moment it opened part way. Toby could hear quiet whispers, then Lady Laura nodded and walked back over to them,

"Lady Zelda will be right with you," then she disappeared out the main door.

Toby looked around the room, it was painted a dull greenish-grey with no pictures or other wall hangings to brighten it up. There was one window in the back of the room that looked out onto the back of another drab looking building that appeared to be some sort of warehouse. The only other furniture in the room was a small table in one corner with an empty vase on it and a large coat tree sitting in the other corner that had a sweater or something hanging from it. He heard footsteps and looked around.

Lady Zelda walked up to the high back chair and sat down. She looked at them both and smiled

"I'm sure you have lots of questions and I will try to answer them all. Whatever I tell you will be the truth and is not to be discussed with anyone outside these quarters. Will you both agree to that?"

Both answered at the same time, "Yes Mam." "Yes Mam."

"Fine, lets get started."

Toby looked at Rain and was the first to speak. "Why couldn't Rain tell me about her new position?, It really came as a shock."

Rain spoke up, "I'll answer that, I didn't tell you because I didn't know about it myself. All I knew was that there were going to be some changes in the leadership in our community and I wanted to be back here in time for the town's meeting so I could find out what they were. I feel it's important to know what's going on in our community first hand, and not being told about it after the fact by someone who probably don't have their facts straight."

Lady Zelda nodded her head, "That's correct, Rain had no idea she had been chosen to replace Lady Laura as the new Junior aide. The final decision was made after we learned that you had rescued her safely from the hidden temple. I don't believe that anyone except the quorum knew that I was stepping down to an advisory position only, leaving the position open that Rain was selected for."

Toby thought for a moment, "Isn't she kind of young for such an important position?, I'll be sixteen in a couple of months and she is three or four months younger than me. Has she reached the age of accountability yet?"

"Oh Yes" Zelda paused, "It was unanimous with the quorum of twelve that she was trustworthy and mentally capable to handle her new task. She also comes from a very special linage. I'm going to tell you both about Rains ancestry that has been kept a secret for her own protection, however I believe the secret must be out now, that's why Dr. Zodd chose her to be sacrificed."

Chapter 24

The Linage

Zelda leaned back in her chair, looked at the two curious youngsters sitting in front of her, then started. "Toby, you remember the first time you visited Djuppland and I told you how it was believed that witches came to this land to avoid being persecuted in your land?" Toby Nodded. "Well what I told you wasn't just a story or theory, what I told you was documented fact. I gave you some names of the original thirteen who learned the secret of the connecting corridor and were able to cross over to this land, including Dr. Zodd and Crabby Abbey." Toby nodded again.

"Well after several years Abbey started missing some of her family, and with Dr. Zodd's approval she crossed back through the corridor to her homeland, then returned with her two daughters, Jewel and Crystal. "They had both grown up to be beautiful young women. Jewel had dark hair and green eyes, Crystal had blond hair and blue eyes. When Dr. Zodd saw Jewel he was smitten by her beauty and announced that he was officially changing her name to the Emerald Princess and would make her his bride on the night of the first full moon in June. To keep her from running off he locked her in his secret temple that he had forced the giants to build, and would hold her there to await the union and mating of the two on the selected date."

"Jewel hatted the Dr. with his sinister ways and dreaded becoming his slave/wife to be totally controlled by him. Back in her homeland she had attended a school for higher learning and had been fascinated with Greek Methodology, especially the story of the minotaur, a gruesome half beast, half man that was an evil, cannibalistic creature. It lived in a dark maze inside a mountain and would kill and eat anyone who entered the maze. "That is why Dr Zodd created it. He planned to give it to Jewel as a wedding gift and hopefully soften her feelings towards him."

Zelda paused, "You know the rest of the story," "Rather than become Dr Zodd's bride she sacrificed herself to the minotaur on the eve of their wedding day. "Dr Zodd blamed Abbey and Crystal for Jewels hatred towards him and demanded they be brought before him for punishment. Abbey helped Jewel to flee to Duppland, then changed her name and disappeared somewhere in the vast wastelands of Azzure. Crystal went on to marry someone in Duppland, Had a daughter named Iris, who grew up, married and had a daughter named Margo," she looked at Rain and smiled, "Who happens to be your mother. That makes you the only living descendant of Abbey who was called Crabby Abbey by her friends as a joke. She was really a very pleasant, passionate, nice looking woman. I'm guessing that's where Rain gets her pleasant disposition and good looks from." Rain smiled and blushed a little.

"Anyway, she is the only living descendant of Abbey and we believe that is why she was chosen to be the first human sacrifice to the minotaur. Dr Zodd believes that if all of Abbeys living descendants are disposed of it will ease his grieving of many, many, many years for his beloved emerald princess. Some believe that his grieving has made him the evil warlock that he has become." Zelda looked at Rain, "Well young lady, I hope this has answered some of the many questions you have about your mother, and why Boggs was unable to answer them for you."

Zelda looked at Toby, "I forgot about Boggs, do you know where he is?"

Toby thought for a moment, "Yes, I believe he is walking home to take a nap, he's almost there now. He's carrying his old walking stick and whistling." Rain looked at toby and smiled. Toby looked around surprised.

"How did I know all that?"

Chapter 25

What To believe

Zelda looked at Toby and smiled, "When I held both of your hands earlier I was able to pass some of my telepathic abilities to you. I felt that you knew enough about some of our people and about our ways that you would use this ability to see things in your mind constructively." Toby thought for a moment.

"So is everyone here in Duppland a witch?"

Zelda shook her head, "That depends on what you think makes a witch. If you believe that all witches are evil and do bad things, then by your definition, no one here is a witch."

Toby thought for a moment, "I have met several people here that I know have special powers, and they all seem to use them for the good of others. There's Master Boggs, Master Diggers, Lady Laura, and of course you. I also met a lady named Ashley who was over four hundred years old. She said she was one of the original thirteen who first passed through the portal. She helped me locate the stairway to the temple, gave me some food and a beautiful silver-blue cape. She said she was the tailor for Dr Zodd but snuck out of his compound because he had gotten so mean and evil. She was very nice to me. The only witches I hear bad things about are the ones I have never met or seen."

Zelda looked into Toby's eyes, "You've been visiting Duppland, or should I say Rain for almost two years now. You know about our way of life and our beliefs. You know that some of us have special powers that the other members of our community don't have. So, you must have determined by now that a few of us are true witches, am I correct?"

Toby nodded, "After my experience with the walking stick that the four of you put some sort of a spell on, and the living stone creature that was created by Dr Zodd, I knew there had to be some supernatural powers to do these things. So yes, I definitely know that both good and evil witches are living here."

Toby continued, "What about that unicorn that came to our rescue, did you place some sort of spell on it so it would rescue us?"

Zelda laughed and shook her head, "No, not at all, I simply asked it to."

"Whaaat!," "You know how to speak unicorn talk?"

Zelda laughed again, "No, neither of us can speak the others language, but there are other ways to communicate with animals. When this unicorn was very young it was found over by the cemetery, probably looking for its mother. Master Diggers figured it had lost its mother some way and was orphaned. The poor little thing was hungry, scared and all alone. Master Diggers contracted the quorum of twelve and each of them took turns caring for it. They all tried to communicate with it without any success. One of the members of the quorum decided to try using mental communication with it. It started to understand thoughts like, come here, lay down, where are you." The quorum members started to mentally understand its thoughts like I'm hungry, I'm over here, pet me and other small things."

"The animal stayed with the quorum for over a year. During that time they learned to carry on complete mental conversations with each other. Even at a distance. When it was time for it to return to the forest to find a mate and friends of his own kind he thanked everyone and told us if he could ever do anything for us to let him know. When I told him about your situation telepathically he volunteered to go. This type of communicating works really well with him, he even let me know when he found you and was on his way back. I've often wondered why scientist in your world don't try it with dolphins, they seem to be very friendly with humans." Toby shrugged.

Zelda leaned back in her chair, "Well I've been sitting here talking a lot, or as Rain calls it "Gibber-Jabber," now we need to get to the main point. As I told you I passed on some of my telepathic ability to you. It probably won't do much for you back in Brighton, however you should find it quite helpful when you visit here. I also gave you some of my visionary perception ability. You'll will need to work on that, it takes practice to perfect it."

Toby looked puzzled, "Just what is that?"

"It's the ability to see in your mind what someone is planning for you, good or bad. You can mentally know when someone is planning to harm you before it happens, Zelda paused for a moment, "Now here's something you must remember, Dr Zodd will not be pleased with you. You destroyed his stone monster and defeated the giant guard at the back entrance to the maze. I'm sure he will be planning some sort of retaliation for you and Rain. "You must also realize that evil doings or black magic as it is often called is much more powerful than the good magic we practice here. Also remember that Dr Zodd has had over four hundred years to perfect his powers. I've heard that he can levitate, you know, float up in the air, disappear at will, perform out of body excursions and has perfected mind over matter, that's how he created the living stone monster. He is not someone to be taken lightly."

Toby shuddered, "Doesn't the silver sword keep him out of Duppland?"

Zelda shook her head, "No, just his army of giants, he uses them to fight his battles."

Rain spoke up, "Well if he does show up here, there should be enough of us to overpower his evil magic and he will have to leave or be destroyed."

Zelda nodded, "Lets hope so."

Toby and Rain said their farewells to Lady Zelda and left the office. Zelda returned to her private room, pulled three or four leaves from a plant by the window, dropped them in a cup and poured hot water over them. She then sat down in a comfortable chair, her tea in her hand and smiled. Through the window next to her chair she could see the young couple as they walked back towards the picnic area, playfully shoving each other every so often and laughing. Zelda thought, "What a wonderful young lady my great, great, great granddaughter is growing up to be."

Chapter 26

A Farewell Kiss

Toby and Rain sat down on a bench under a shade tree and looked at each other. Toby was the first to speak,

"Wow" "If everything Lady Zelda says is true, maybe Dr. Zodd will again try to avenge you for being "just you."

Rain smiled a little, "Well here in Duppersville he can't do much, there is too many of us to ward off his evil powers, and he knows that. I do believe however that she has serious concerns about him trying to avenge you along with us. That's probably why she passed on some of her visionary perception powers to you, so you would know in advance if some evil scheme is being cooked up for you. You will need to work on that, it can be kind of fun once you get the hang of it."

Toby nodded, "Yeah, I will", then he looked at his watch, reached over and took a dead leaf that had fallen into Rains hair and flicked it away.

They sat quietly for a few minutes thinking about all that had happened in the last six days and gazing at nothing off in the distance. Toby stood up with a sad look on his face,

"It seems like the good days go by fast and the bad ones go slow, This has been a good day but I need to leave and head back home. I promised my parents I would do some things around the house and they will probably be back home sometime tomorrow."

Rain looked at Toby, "I wish you didn't need to go, I'll really miss you." Toby took a step back and cocked his head,

"A Lot?",

"Yeah, a whole lot."

"Well that's good," "That little curse you put on me two years ago is still baffling me. I'll be doing something important like flying my model drone or something and you pop into my head."

Rain smiled, "Glad I got it right."

"Yeah," "me to I guess, Oh, by the way, I left some things at your house, the cape Ashpit Ashley gave me, the water flask I got from the old hermit of hidden gulch and the walking stick your grandfather gave me. Will you take care of them for me?, they mean a lot to me."

She nodded, "Of corse I will, They all mean a lot to me too. They all helped save our bacon a couple of times back on the trail."

Toby got a funny look on his face, "Where did you ever come up with that saying," "Saved our bacon?" "It sounds like you didn't eat all your breakfast."

She laughed, "It sounds better than saying "Saved our rears," doesn't it?"

He nodded, "Yeah, I guess so."

He took Rain by the hand, "Are you going to walk me to the tree?"

Rain nodded, "I really don't want to but I guess I will. Maybe you can come back in a couple of weeks and we can do something exciting."

Toby shook his head, "It can't get much more exciting than the week we just had." They both laughed and started walking towards the tree and the portal that would take Toby back to Brighton and his home.

They stood under the tree for a few minutes thinking about the past few days. Rain took one of Toby's hands in both hers, "Thank you again for rescuing me, no one else would have been able to do what you did and you will always be my hero. Toby smiled a little and looked down,

"It made me feel good that you and Zelda put your faith in me. It almost all seems like a dream, but I guess it wasn't, because here we are saying good-by." Rains eyes looked wet, "Yeah, we've been saying good-by a lot lately," then she stood on her toes and gave Toby a quick little kiss on his lips, "don't forget to think about me" she whispered.

Toby smiled and nodded, he had never been kissed by a girl before. He was still smiling after he passed through th portal and back to the park and oak tree behind his house. He looked around, the sun was sinking low in the western sky. He started up the hill to his home and a weeks chores to do in one day.

"Beep' "Beep" "Beep", Toby had sat his alarm for six A M and it went off right on time. He moaned a couple of times, hit the snooze button and laid there for ten more minutes. Finally he slowly climbed out of bed, stretched and staggered into the bathroom. He washed his face, combed his hair and brushed his teeth then stood looking at his face in the mirror and rubbing his chin. "Well" he said out loud, "You'll probably be shaving before too long," then in s lower voice mumbled, "Don't know if that's a good thing or not." He shrugged his shoulders, got dressed and made his way down the stairs and into the kitchen. He poured himself a heaping bowl of cereal, covered it with cold milk and sat down to his morning feast. Cereal was one of the things he really missed in Duppland. No one there ever ate it. He thought maybe he would take a couple of boxes with him the next time he went, then maybe he would be the towns hero again without having to risk his life.

He rinsed off his bowl and spoon, placed them in the dishwasher and headed out to the garage. He raised the overhead door, picked up the six newspapers that were laying in front of it and placed them neatly inside next to the container marked recycle. He stood there for a moment looking at the lawnmower that seemed to be laughing at him. He did not like mowing the lawn and jokingly had tried to get his dad to buy a goat to keep it short. Behind the lawnmower stood an array of long handled garden tools lined up neatly against the wall.

Toby shook his head, grabbed the mower and headed out to the lush green lawn that must have grown at least a foot while he was gone. Finally, after what seemed like hours of mowing the huge expanse of green, Toby pushed the tired lawnmower up onto the driveway, rinsed it off with the hose, then pushed it back to its resting place to await its next use. Next he selected a long handled rake and garden hoe and headed to the garden behind the house to attack the weeds and other unwanted things with the weapons he had chosen.

He finished in the garden quicker than he thought. The ground was nice and damp from the sprinkler system that came on during the night, making it easy to remove the weeds and other unwanted stubble without too much effort. He knocked the bits of damp soil from his sneakers, rinsed off the rake and hoe, sat them back in their resting place behind the lawnmower and closed the overhead door.

He stood there for a couple of minutes surveying his handy work, then said out loud, "Well", It looks good." He glanced at his watch, it read five after three. His mom had said they would be home today sometime between four and five. He nodded his head, went inside the house, laid down on the sofa and closed his eyes. He laid there thinking, "This is exactly how I was when everyone left," then dozed off.

"Hello," "Hello," "Anyone home?"

Toby sat up and rubbed his eyes, Heather and his mom were coming through the front door, both pulling some luggage behind them. His mom looked at him.

"Can you run out and grab your dads suitcase, He dropped us off then headed to the car wash to try and clean some of the bugs off the car. She always called it a car even though it was a SUV. Toby nodded and hastefully, went out and grabbed the large suitcase and carried it up the stairs to his parents bedroom. When he came back down, his mom who was looking out the front window, turned and walked over to Toby and gave him a big hug.

"The lawn and garden look great, and the house looks just as good as it did when we left. And to think I was worried about leaving you here by yourself to take care of things." She gave him a couple of pats on the back then headed upstairs to start unpacking. Toby walked over to the couch and sat down next to Heather, "Well," "Are you going to tell me how your cheer team did in New Orleans?"

Heather grinned, "You bet," "We finished second and that was really good considering there were over thirty teams in the competition. Our coach received a beautiful trophy and we all got jerseys with our teams logo on them. Our coach says if we work really hard we could be the national champions next year. It was a great trip." Heather took a drink from a can of soda she was holding, "Well" "Did you do anything exciting or just lay around all week wearing out the couch?"

Toby grinned, "Actually I had quite an exciting week. I was whisked off to a far away land where I was needed to rescue a young princess who was being held in a lost temple and was to be sacrificed to an evil stone monster."

"After rescuing her and destroying the stone monster I defeated a huge giant with only three blows who was guarding the way out of the temple. I also had to slay a dragon using just my walking stick, then the young princess and I rode back to her homeland on a beautiful white unicorn where we received a hero's welcome. Now here I am back home again, safe and sound."

Heather sat there shaking her head, "You really need to quit playing so many video games, you're starting to fantasize yourself as being the hero in them."

Toby grinned, "Welllll" "No matter what you think, you're still my favorite sister, and by the way, I like your new jeans."

Heather thought for a moment, "That's because I'm your only sister and believe me, I'll get even with you for these jeans, I had to pay for them myself, you jerk." They both laughed.

Printed in the United States
By Bookmasters